PURELY ACADEMIC

The rise and fall of Charles Mittleman

DAVID ABRAMSON

with Michelle Schusterman

David Abramson

PURELY ACADEMIC

Forward

This work began as a play and was first performed at the University of Oxford, UK, in 2013. The performance was directed by Dr Dimitrina Spencer as part of a workshop entitled "Thriving in Research and Professional Collaborations: a Collaborative Learning Lab".

It was then significantly edited and reworked, under the critical guidance of Alix Phelan, who helped shape the dialogue and focus. It was staged again as part of the 2017 eResearch conference in Brisbane, Australia, to an audience of IT academics. Along the way there were a number of staged readings at the University of Queensland, organised and promoted by Dr Sue O'Brien, and also the University of California, San Diego, organised and promoted by Drs Michael Kalichman and Emily Roxworthy. These were cast by senior colleagues at the University of Queensland and actors in San Diego.

In 2021 I decided to convert the play text to a novella and instigated a collaboration with Michelle Schusterman. As a ghostwriter Michelle is often invisible. However, this was a genuine collaboration, so she is named as a co-author. How could I do otherwise for a work which discusses plagiarism and academic ethics? Michelle preserved most of the dialogue in the original script, and used her significant skills to augment it with nuance and detail; like colouring a black and white photo. I am eternally in her debt and in awe of her skills.

Purely Academic has many uses, either as a play or a novella. We hope you enjoy it.

DISCLAIMER

This is a work of fiction. Names, characters, places and incidents either are products of the author's imagination or are used fictitiously. Any resemblance to actual events or locales or persons, living or dead, is entirely coincidental.

Front cover credits: Clinton Ward, iStockPhoto.com

First Printing, 2021

To my wife Heather,
and daughters Rebecca, Sarah and
Elizabeth

For them, this work was not purely
academic.

Chapter 1

Professor John Holywell was in desperate need of a double espresso.

He repeated the order in his mind as he navigated the halls of Twin Lakes College. *Double espresso, one Equal.* A quick stop to meet a PhD student—a rather reluctant promise he'd made to a colleague at the meeting this morning—and he'd be off to the café.

Holywell spotted room 202 and sighed. For the briefest of moments, he considered passing by without knocking. "Sorry, Tim," he would say later in his office, phone receiver cradled between his shoulder and ear, coffee securely in hand. "I dropped by, but the boy wasn't there."

But Holywell wasn't the type to lie, not even to a colleague he'd only met once or twice. Telling the littlest of white lies caused him to sweat, and worse, to giggle like a schoolgirl. A high-pitched titter that a few of his fellow professors often teased him about. Embarrassing, really. Especially on the rare occasion when it happened around a student.

And so he knocked on the door to room 202 without an inkling as to how much he would later come to regret it.

"Yes?" called a voice inside.

Holywell pushed the door open and poked his head inside the small office. "I'm looking for Charles?"

The gangly boy seated behind the desk sprang up like a jack-in-the-box. "That's me, yes, Charles Mittleman!" He rushed forward to grasp Holywell's hand and all but yank him fully into the room. "You must be Professor Holywell? Thanks for coming."

Holywell attempted a smile as he regained his balance. "I was on campus anyway."

"My supervisor, Dr. Henderson, has told me all about you." Charles ran his fingers through his straw-colored hair, causing it to stick up in all directions. "All good things, of course."

"Tim? Did he really?" Holywell replied, slightly bemused. Tim had been almost apologetic when he'd asked Holywell to introduce himself to Charles before he left the campus. "How nice. So I hear you want to come and study with me at Northwest?"

"Yes, yes. Come in, won't you?"

But Holywell hovered near the doorway. "Do you mind if we go to the café? I'm dying for a coffee, and—"

"Lisa*? Lisa!"* Charles bellowed, causing Holywell to reel back a bit in shock. He turned as a young brunette appeared in the doorway behind him.

"Yes, Charles? What is it now?" Her voice had an edge that Charles appeared not to notice.

"Professor Holywell wants coffee."

More than a little mortified, Holywell raised his hands. "Ah, no, I don't mind going down to the café!"

Charles waved dismissively. "Lisa's very happy to serve such an eminent professor. What type of coffee do you want?"

"Oh, Charles, I don't think I deserve such—"

"Professor Holywell wants a flat white," Charles told Lisa. "And a sugar bun."

Holywell pinched the bridge of his nose as Lisa headed down the hall. "Ah, since you insist, I'd prefer a double espresso!" he called weakly. "But it's not...not necessary..."

"No problem, no problem at all." Charles headed back to the desk and sat. "The other students love to help me."

"Really?" Holywell pictured Lisa's expression, which could only be described as lethal, and cleared his throat. He pulled up the chair in front of the desk, his gaze falling on the daily calendar featuring a vaguely familiar cartoon character. The date read April 1st, 1997, and Holywell blinked. April Fool's Day. He hadn't realized.

"So," he said, clearing his throat. "Tim is your PhD supervisor. Why do you want to come and work with me?"

Charles rolled his eyes. "He's *leaving.* I've only been here a year, and—"

"Leaving. Really?" Holywell leaned forward, interested. "Where's he going?"

"Moonshine Systems. He says he's had enough of academia."

"Moonshine!" Holywell exclaimed. "That's quite a coup for them."

Charles ignored this. "But he said you'd be a perfect supervisor. And I think Northwest University would be a much better fit for me anyway."

"Hmm." Holywell frowned slightly. "Aren't there others here who would like to work with you?"

"Yes, of course. But Dr. Henderson said you're the best."

The boy hadn't blinked in several seconds. His eyes were locked on Holywell with a laser focus that was more than a little unnerving.

Holywell coughed. "Ah, well, I'd have to talk to Tim about that..."

"Your software, Triggle? It's very well known."

Despite his discomfort, Holywell sat up a little straighter. He'd begun working on Triggle in early 1996, and in just two years, his team had made great strides.

"Yes, it is," he said proudly. "But you must've made quite a start already! What are you working on?"

It was Charles' turn to sit up and square his shoulders. Excitement flashed in his eyes.

"I'm working on the Internet."

This proclamation was met with silence.

Holywell nodded, silently encouraging the boy to continue. But Charles merely beamed at him. He suddenly seemed so guileless, so *young,* that Holywell had to smile.

"Ah," he said, trying to hide his amusement. "Well, that's a pretty broad topic. What in particular?"

Charles shrugged at this utterly inconsequential question. "I haven't exactly locked it down yet. I just think the Internet's going to revolutionize life."

"Mmm. How so?"

"I don't know." Charles began jiggling his right leg, coins rattling in his pocket. "I just get the impression it's going to make a big difference."

Holywell was starting to understand why Tim had been so apologetic when he'd asked Holywell to drop by and introduce himself to Charles.

"I see." Holywell settled back in his chair and regarded the boy. He was passionate, that much was clear. Perhaps he just needed stronger guidance. Northwest had an excellent graduate program, but it wasn't really known for its research or PhD programs. Charles Mittleman might be somewhat...abrasive, to put it mildly, but Holywell had dealt with all sorts of egos at Northwest University. It was unavoidable when you worked with young people who were too smart for their own good.

Holywell cleared his throat again. "The thing is, Charles, you need to focus on something specific. A PhD is supposed to be an original and significant contribution. Hasn't Dr. Henderson helped you refine your topic?"

Charles let out a derisive snort. "Oh yes, he's made quite a few suggestions. But I'm worried that they're too niche. I want to have a global impact." He swiveled around and plucked a small blue hardcover off the bookshelf. "I've already produced a book, actually."

That got Holywell's attention. "You've written a book?"

"Yeah." Charles held the book out, and Holywell accepted it. "I wrote to a whole bunch of leading scientists and asked them to write a chapter."

Holywell was so preoccupied studying the cover—in particular, the words *by Charles Mittleman* embossed in gold along the bottom—that it took a beat for him to register what Charles had just said. He glanced up, finding himself once again bemused by the boy's earnest gaze.

"You asked them to...ah." Holywell arched an eyebrow. "So you haven't actually *written* a book."

"I've collated their work," Charles said, as if the two things were synonymous. "I want to be a thought leader in this area."

Holywell struggled not to smirk. "You might need to do a little thinking yourself."

Charles nodded. "When can I come and work with you?"

"Ah, well," Holywell said, his smile vanishing. His eyes darted over to the door. "Like I said, I'll need to speak to Tim. And you'll need to get a scholarship. And—"

"Where's that damn girl with your coffee?" Charles shot up and bounded to the door, leaving Holywell speechless behind him. "Lisa? *Lisa*!"

Lisa appeared a moment later. Though she handed

Charles a paper cup without a word, the venomous look in her eyes caused Holywell to wince. Charles, however, did not appear to notice. He closed the door in Lisa's face, swiveled around, and presented Holywell with the cup.

"Flat white," Holywell said, gazing down at the milky contents. "Just what the doctor ordered."

Charles returned to his seat. "Dr. Henderson's already agreed to let me go if you'll take me."

Holywell choked slightly on his coffee. "Ah. But what about a topic?"

"I've read some of your papers on Internet search.'

"Yes, but what did *you* have in mind?"

For the first time, Charles appeared unsure. He swallowed, his Adam's apple visibly bobbing. "Perhaps you can suggest some topics?"

Sighing, Holywell set his flat white on the desk.

"Well, the Internet's useless if you can't find what you want. Triggle helps you find all of the sites that match your query. Imagine one day when all the world's information is on the Internet, and you have a question."

Charles was nodding vigorously. "Yes, yes?" The gleam of hunger in his eyes was more than a little unsettling, but Holywell continued.

"You'll be able to type that in and Triggle will return the answers." Holywell began to warm to his topic. In truth, he could happily talk about Triggle for hours on end. Particularly with someone who could appreciate the finer details. "We've got some of the ideas worked out, but you could carve out a project developing them further. It's very early days in Internet search, so it would be pretty easy to make a contribution."

"I'd love working on that!" Charles exclaimed. He looked like a man who'd just been handed the keys to the castle.

Holywell pressed his lips together, wishing he could take the words back. His palms were beginning to sweat. It was time to end this meeting.

"Yes, well, I'm not making any promises," he said a touch too loudly, wiping his hands on his trousers as he stood up. "I'll speak to Dr. Henderson. If your CV stacks up and you get a scholarship, I'll *consider* supervising you."

Charles grasped his hand and shook it hard, grinning from ear to ear.

"It'll be great working together."

Holywell opened his mouth, fully intending to gently correct the boy, then thought better of it.

"Yes," he said instead. "Yes, it will."

And he was utterly helpless to stop the high-pitched giggle that followed.

Chapter 2

The breeze that whipped across the Northwest courtyard bordered on warm, and the students gathering around the fountain were shrugging off their jackets and tilting their faces up to the sun. Holywell loved this time of year in Seattle, when the sky was bright blue and the mountains were visible in the distance—shockingly so, after months of hiding behind fog and clouds. He picked up the pace as he headed for the technology building, whistling to himself.

"John?"

Holywell turned to see Professor Mary Long entering through the glass double doors, holding a stack of folders. She wore a crisp blue blouse the exact color of sky and navy trousers. "Mary! Where'd you come from?"

She laughed, her warm brown eyes twinkling. "I was waving at you from the fountain, but you had your head in the clouds."

"I booked my flight this morning," Holywell said cheerfully, and the two fell into step side by side. "Two weeks in Santa Monica, nothing to worry about but sunscreen and sangria."

"Sounds amazing," Mary replied, adjusting the folders as they headed up the stairs. "When do you leave?"

"Next Monday. How about you?"

"Not till the end of July." Mary shot him a grin. "Rome will be worth the wait, though."

"Rome!" Holywell exclaimed. "Now that's a vacation. What is all that?" he added, pointing to the folders.

"I finally ranked the scholarship applications." Mary followed Holywell into his office, setting the stack down on his desk. She flipped open the top folder. "This guy Mittleman looks pretty good."

Holywell struggled not to roll his eyes. "Yes, he seems good."

"Why does he want to leave Twin Lakes?"

"Henderson's leaving, so Mittleman's looking for a new supervisor." Holywell took the application Mary held out to him with a sigh. "I'm a little worried about his progress to date."

"Why?"

"He just hasn't achieved much."

Mary came to stand next to him, gazing at Charles Mittleman's application. "He's just completed a book on the Internet. It pushed him up the ranking quite a lot."

"But all he's really done is bring people together!" Holywell exclaimed. "It's their ideas and they do the writing. He just puts his name on the book."

Mary smirked. "I'd normally expect that from a much more senior academic." She nudged Holywell with her elbow, and he cracked a smile.

"He seems to have people all organized to help

him." Holywell paused, remembering. "You know, when I visited him last week and suggested we go get a coffee, he snapped his fingers and literally ordered another PhD student to go a get it! I've never seen anything like it."

"So he's a bit overzealous," Mary replied. "Who wasn't at that age?"

Holywell chuckled. "Well, that's a good point. I was downright arrogant."

"You? No." Mary placed a hand to her chest in mock surprise.

"Alright, alright." Holywell settled into his chair, his gaze straying back to the stack of applications. "You know, maybe I *am* being too hard on the boy. I certainly thought I was going to change the world, back when I was a PhD. Wills was constantly knocking me down a few pegs."

"Wills?"

"Oh, a supervisor I had," Holywell told her. "A bit scary, but brilliant. He was a mentor of sorts."

"Maybe you can play Wills to this kid's Holywell," Mary said with a grin, tapping Mittleman's application.

Holywell leaned back in his chair. "I don't know..."

"Come on, John. On paper, his credentials look too good to pass up. We don't often see students with a transcript like that! All those papers so early on in his career."

"I suppose," Holywell admitted. "I'll tell you what. He's so good at organizing others, he can supervise me and I'll go back to being a student. I think the pay and conditions are better."

Mary laughed as she headed for the door. "Be careful what you wish for, John."

* * *

In a cramped studio apartment above a dive bar and across the street from a shuttered experimental theater, Charles Mittleman tossed his briefcase on the floor and began ranting at his cat.

"It's been two weeks, Sophie. Can you believe this?" He marched over to his desk as he spoke, powering on his Packard Bell desktop. "I mean, I thought Northwest was a respectable university. I thought they had a *competent* staff, unlike Twin Lakes. How long does it take to approve an application?"

Sophie flicked her tail in response, a few stray ginger hairs falling to the carpet.

Charles' stomach growled, and he glanced at his watch. It was nearly five—had he eaten lunch today? No, Charles realized suddenly, he'd been too busy researching.

Annoyed, he yanked open the refrigerator door. A few brown bananas, a carton of Sunny D, and a container of something from Royal Wok. Charles frowned, trying to remember when he'd last ordered take out. Last week, he was pretty sure. This week, he'd mostly dined at the cafeteria at Twin Lakes, staying increasingly late hours.

Charles grabbed the container and took a sniff at

the congealed sesame chicken inside. Didn't smell lethal. He found a plastic fork in a drawer where he kept the take out menus and began to pace as he ate it cold. (His kitchen hadn't come with a microwave, and the oven was far too blackened on the inside for him to risk turning it on.)

Charles had only lived here for a year. It was cheap enough, and besides, he wasn't planning on living here forever. Charles Mittleman was made for bigger and better things. This was just a stop along the way to greatness, which was why he hadn't bothered with things like furniture beyond a pull-out futon and a single bookcase.

And his desk, of course—the largest and most important piece of furniture in the room. It was pushed against the only window in his apartment, which faced the apartment building next door. He could see straight into the living room of the woman who lived opposite him, a cheery middle-aged blonde who enjoyed working out with Jane Fonda every day precisely at seven pm. She waved at him occasionally, and Charles suspected she would try to chat with him if his window was ever open, which was why he never opened it.

A beep brought Charles' attention back to his desktop. He crossed the room quickly and opened Internet Explorer, listening to the dial-up shrieks and *pings* as he shoved another forkful of chicken into his mouth.

"I checked my email at least a hundred times today,

and nothing," he muttered, setting the container down and logging into his account. *No new messages.* Charles scowled, straightening up. "I'm telling you, Sophie, sometimes I think everyone is—"

Ring-ring!

Charles fell silent, blinking in surprise. It had been so long since his phone had rung, he'd almost forgotten he had one. Dropping the container and fork on his desk, he flew across the room, causing Sophie to leap onto the futon with a hiss, and snatched the receiver off the phone that sat on the kitchen counter. "Charles Mittleman," he said as loudly and confidently as he could.

"Yes, Charles? Professor Holywell here."

Charles gripped the receiver tighter. "Yes, sir! Did you get my messages?"

A muffled cough. "Well, yes, of course. There were quite a lot of them. Look, I just wanted to let you know that your transfer is officially approved, and we've arranged a scholarship for this fall."

"Fall?" Charles's elation vanished. "Is there any reason it has to take that long? I was thinking this month."

For a moment, he thought Holywell had disconnected. Then the professor let out another cough. "That's, um...well, Charles, that's not really possible, especially right before summer break. All new PhD students will start this fall."

"Can't you make an exception?" Charles pressed. "I'd really like to—"

"Afraid not," Holywell interrupted, his voice raised. "I'm looking forward to working with you this fall, Charles. Have a nice summer."

Click.

Charles hung up and headed back to his desk. He used the plastic fork to scrape the spilled sesame chicken back into the container.

"Well, I'm in," he told Sophie. "Of course. They know a good thing when they see it. But I have to wait for fall to transfer. Can you believe it?"

Sophie stared at him, her amber eyes glowing with righteous indignation. Charles shoveled another fork-ful of chicken in his mouth and stared at his desktop, his mind speeding ahead. He might have to wait until fall to start at Northwest, but that didn't mean the summer was a waste.

He had work to do.

Chapter 3

Holywell shook his umbrella vigorously before ducking inside the technology building. He made his way to the office, clutching his double espresso and waving to a few colleagues down the hall.

Joanne, one of Holywell's brightest software developers, was waiting outside his door, hand on her protruding belly. She wore a loose-fitting blouse with a pattern of tiny daffodils and stylish black maternity pants that flared slightly at the ankle.

"John! How was Santa Monica?" she asked as he unlocked the door.

Holywell sighed, flipping on the light switch. "Bliss. I should've stayed another two weeks...I'm already losing my tan! How was your vacation?"

"Oh, you know, very glamorous," she said wryly, lowering herself into a chair. "Lying on the couch eating Doritos, watching Seinfeld reruns, and gestating this critter."

Holywell chuckled. "When are you due?"

"Still a few months to go." Joanne tucked a stray curl behind her ear. "I can't wait for this to be over."

"You should have some long nighttime coding sessions coming up when the baby comes."

"Cobra by nursery light, hey?"

Holywell laughed. “Something like that.”

A knock came at the door. Before Holywell could respond, it flew open and Charles Mittleman strode into his office. Holywell struggled to keep the smile on his face, trying not to think of the dozens of emails Charles had sent him over the summer—only a few of which Holywell had responded to.

“Ah, Charles! I want to introduce you to our most senior programmer, Joanne. She’s done all of the software development so far. I really think she’s looking forward to some help.”

Charles was nodding vigorously. “Joanne, great to meet you. Can’t wait to contribute to Triggle. What language is it written in?”

“Cobra,” Joanne replied. “Do you know it?”

“No, but I’ve written a book on Basic. You know Basic, right?”

Holywell winced, but Joanne looked amused. “It was the first language I learned in high school. But I’ve been using Cobra for about five years. I’m sure you’ll pick it up fast en—”

“Professor, couldn’t we switch to Basic?” Charles said, turning to Holywell. “That’d suit me better.”

Joanne’s eyebrows shot up, and Holywell cleared his throat.

“Charles, you’ll need to learn Cobra. But we’re getting a little ahead of ourselves. I need you to do some reading and then we can discuss your topic in more detail. And you’ll need to access all of our papers.”

More nodding. Holywell couldn’t help but think

that the boy looked like a marionette whose master had lost control of the strings.

"Okay, okay." Charles glanced at Joanne. "Hey, unless there was anything else you need, I've got a few admin things to sort out with Prof."

Joanne stared at him incredulously, and Holywell pinched the bridge of his nose.

"Charles—"

"No, no, it's fine." Joanne heaved herself out of the chair. "I'll leave you both to it."

Once the door was closed behind her, Charles took her chair. His gaze was not on Holywell, but on the window behind his desk. On a day like today, the view was nothing more than foggy gray skies. But on a sunny day, Mt. Rainier would emerge in all its snow-capped glory. Holywell was always amazed by its appearance. It was so easy to forget the mountain was lurking out there in the fog and clouds.

"Um, so, the room you've allocated for me," Charles said. "There are three other people in there already, and no windows."

Holywell tried to keep his voice even. "That's pretty standard. What's the problem?"

"I've got a lot more experience than the other students," Charles said pointedly, as if this were the most obvious fact in the world.

"You're all PhD students to me, and you all have the same rights," Holywell said. "You'll just have to manage. Was there something else?"

"I need business cards."

Holywell couldn't quite stop the little *harumph* that escaped his throat. "We don't usually allocate business cards for PhD students."

"I travel to conferences quite a lot, and I need to have business cards. Isn't that standard?"

"I've never had a PhD ask for them before, to be honest."

"Would it be possible for them to say I'm a Research Fellow? The cards?"

"No. Assuming I get you some, they would say you're a PhD student, because that's what you are."

"But surely it's the same thing. Research Fellow sounds much better."

"Yes," Holywell replied with a smile. "It actually is much better."

Charles stared at him blankly for a moment. Before he could respond, Joanne poked her head in.

"If you two are about done, I did have a few things I wanted to catch you up on, John..."

Holywell waved her in. "Charles was just leaving."

But Charles didn't vacate the chair. "I've started a paper. I'm nearly done, in fact."

Holywell gaped at him. "You...what?"

"I emailed you weeks ago. I told you."

"Yes, and if I recall, I responded to that email and told you to do some thinking first."

Charles continued as if Holywell hadn't spoken. "It's on Triggle's features."

Joanne caught Holywell's eye, then turned to Charles. "But they've already appeared in our previous papers. It's not ethical to publish the same work twice, Charles."

"There's a conference in LA that I want to attend," Charles told Holywell, ignoring Joanne completely. "The deadline is this week. I had to get started over the summer."

Holywell struggled to keep his patience. "Have you done anything else? Any other *work*?"

"I got Grace to run some experiments for me."

"Grace?" Holywell repeated.

"Grace Williams, another new PhD," Joanne told him.

"And she doesn't have enough to do without running experiments for other students?"

Joanne arched an eyebrow. "I asked her the same thing. She said it was simpler for her to do the experiments than to train this one up on Cobra."

Holywell took a deep breath. *Patience,* he told himself. The boy was smart. He just needed guidance.

"Joanne, I'm really sorry, but can you give us a few more minutes?"

"No problem."

The moment she left, Charles opened his mouth—but this time, Holywell beat him to it.

"Charles, you need to focus on what *your* contribution is going to be. Your PhD needs to be your own. You can't just spend your time writing papers and ordering other students around!"

"Sure, yeah, I understand," Charles said, head bobbing up and down. "By the way, Professor Levee from the University of Washington has agreed to join my PhD committee."

Holywell was dumbfounded. "Jake Levee? He contacted you?"

"I contacted him."

"You've met him?"

"Not personally," Charles said with a dismissive weave. "He wrote a chapter for my book."

"Charles, we don't *have* PhD committees here."

"No, no, this'll be great for me. Professor Levee is very well known. I think that'll make it easier to get my papers published."

Holywell half-stood, palms flat on his desk. "We don't *have* PhD committees! You should've run this by me first—it's going to be embarrassing now if I have to uninvite him."

Charles shrugged. "Can we just make a committee?"

Holywell sat heavily in his chair and cast his gaze to the ceiling. "Just what we need," he mumbled. "More committees."

"Exactly. Maybe you can contact him. Do you know him?"

"Of course I know him. That's why this is embarrassing." Holywell massaged his temples. He needed to get this conversation back on course. "Look, Charles, forget papers and committees for a moment. What do you know about simulation?"

"Yes."

Holywell blinked. "Simulation?"

"Yes."

They gazed at one another for a moment with twin nonplussed expressions.

"What do you know," Holywell said slowly and deliberately, "about simulation?"

Charles leaned back in his chair and crossed his legs, ankle resting on his knee. "Prof, I do have a first-class degree from the University of Tennessee, you know."

Holywell smiled tightly. "Great. Well, when you come up with some *new* ideas for Triggle, we'll need to simulate them. We can't control the Internet, so we can't do repeatable experiments."

"So what?"

"Anyone in the world should be able to reproduce your work and get the same results."

"But I can just run the real experiments."

"That's my point, Charles," Holywell said, with what he felt was an admirable amount of patience. "You can't just run the real system because you'll get different answers each time."

Charles frowned slightly. "Sorry, I don't get it."

"All right," Holywell said. "Pilots. Pilots train in simulators because it's possible to set up the weather conditions without waiting for the real thing."

"What's this got to do with flying?"

Holywell was not caffeinated enough for this. "Okay, never mind. I need to catch up with Joanne, so we can check in on this later."

He stood, but Charles didn't move.

"You'll contact Professor Levee for me, right?"

Holywell strode toward the door. "I'll contact him."

"And what about my office?" Charles called after him, but Holywell was already halfway down the hall.

Sighing, Charles turned back to the desk. His gaze moved from Holywell's computer to the window behind his desk, which offered a nice view of the courtyard. Then his eyes fell on the phone.

Walking around the desk, Charles knelt down and began pulling open drawers. He found the fat yellow phone book in the bottom drawer and flipped through it until he found the number for The Seattle Daily.

With a grim smile, Charles picked up the receiver and punched in the numbers.

Chapter 4

"He's barely been here a month, Mary," Joanne said. "A *month.*"

Mary Long shook her head and sipped her cappuccino. Across from her, Joanne shifted in her chair, hand on her swollen belly. That morning's issue of The Seattle Times was spread out on the table, peppered with blueberry muffin crumbs.

"Well, he's a go-getter, I'll say that for him," Mary replied, brushing the crumbs away. "Tell you what, I don't want to be there when John sees...ah, speak of the devil."

Joanne looked up as Holywell approached, double espresso in hand. "Good morning, ladies! Mind if I join?"

"Of course not!" Mary smiled at him, shifting her chair to the side as Holywell grabbed one from the next table. She tried to close the paper, but Joanne gave her a gentle kick under the table, followed by a look that clearly said, *he needs to see it.*

"I saw you two having a good laugh while I was ordering," Holywell said cheerfully. "What's the joke?"

"The joke is Charles Mittleman," Joanne told him, "and we're the punchline."

Mary winced as Holywell's smile faltered. "What do you mean?" he asked.

"This was in the paper this morning," Mary told him, tapping the article.

Frowning slightly, Holywell leaned over and read aloud, his voice rising higher in disbelief with every word:

"From his windowless office at Northwest University, Charles Mittleman spearheads an international coalition of computer scientists who want to design search engines for the Internet...what in the world?"

He snatched the paper up and shook it out in front of him, squinting at the words as if hoping he'd read them wrong.

"It only gets worse from there, I'm afraid," Mary said mildly, setting her cup down.

Joanne let out a giggle. "Wait, look, this is my favorite part." She leaned around to see, then pointed at the article. "Look, right here, this quote from Charles...*how can you have vision when you don't have windows*?"

A snort escaped Mary before she could stop it, and her eyes met Joanne's. They burst out laughing at the same time, and Holywell lowered the paper. His expression teetered between disbelief and fury, and Mary bit her lip, trying to wipe the smile from her face.

"That little...he complained about his workspace to me his first day, you know," Holywell said, folding the newspaper in a huff and setting it down. "Having to share with other PhDs. Not having a window. Pushing me for his own office like he's the dean or something."

"And you told him no?" Mary managed to say while keeping a straight face.

Joanne hid her grin behind her cup of herbal tea as Holywell sputtered: "Of course I said no!"

"Well, it seems he thought going to the press would be a good way to pressure you into caving," Mary said. "It's certainly one of the most audacious things a PhD has done in recent memory...and we've had some characters. You said yourself that you were pretty arrogant in your day, didn't you, John?"

Holywell exhaled through his nose. "Nothing like this. I mean, yes, I could be a bit obnoxious at times. I was impatient with anyone who didn't work as fast as I could...I was in such a hurry to get to the finish line, sometimes I rushed the process too much. But Professor Wills always knocked me back in line."

"Charles could use a good knocking," Joanne said with a smile. "He isn't even aware there *is* a line."

"You're right about that." Holywell shook his head, eyeing the newspaper. "I did some boneheaded things, but I never went to the *press.* It's beyond the pale, truly."

"So are you going to confront Charles about it?" Joanne asked.

"I have to, don't I?" Holywell drummed his fingers on the table. "Only...that's what he wants."

"True," Mary said. "Give him an opening, and he'll just bash the door down."

Holywell considered this for a moment. Then he leaned back in his chair and crossed his arms. "Anything I say just goes in one ear and out the other with that boy," he muttered. "Ignoring this—this *article*—that might be the best way to shut Charles Mittleman down."

* * *

True to his word, Holywell didn't mention the article to Charles. But for the next four days, he turned the words over and over again in his mind.

From his windowless office...

Spearheads an international coalition of computer scientists...

The boy was a narcissist, Holywell decided. Delusional. Smart, but not nearly as smart as he thought he was.

A knock at the door interrupted his thoughts. "Yes?"

Mary poked her head in. She hesitated a moment before clearing her throat.

"Have you, um...have you released a new version of Triggle?"

Holywell frowned. "Joanne's working on a new release, but we haven't announced it. Why?"

"I saw something on several news lists." Stepping into the office, Mary closed the door and consulted a sheet of paper. "*The Triggle research group is delighted to announce the latest version of Triggle...*"

"What?" Holywell stood up, stunned.

Mary held up a finger to silence him and continued to read. "*To download a copy please contact the project coordinator, Charles Mittleman.*"

For the briefest of moments, Holywell literally saw red.

"I...this..." He squeezed his eyes closed briefly. "Project *coordinator*? What the hell does he think he's doing? My god, he's only been here five minutes."

"Time flies, doesn't it?" Mary joked half-heartedly.

"He's contributed almost nothing," Holywell went on, his face flushed with anger. "He spends his days bossing the project team around, getting them to do things he should be doing himself. And now he calls himself the project coordinator."

"Perhaps you two need to have a little session," Mary suggested gently.

Holywell snorted. "We've had lots of little *sessions*!"

"I see." Mary gave him an apologetic smile. "I'm glad he's your student, not mine."

"He's just..." Holywell sank back down in his chair, and Mary sat opposite him. He let out a defeated sigh. "He has several publications, but when I looked at the detail, they don't *say* anything."

"And yet, people cite his work."

"Have you seen him interacting with other students in the department?"

Mary nodded. "How does he get people to follow him so easily?"

"It's as if they suspend disbelief," Holywell said.

"You know, he has the best citation count of any of our graduate students, but...well, I can't see why his work would be that important."

"Some of my students told me..." Mary paused, then shrugged. "Well, John, they say Charles has a way of *inflating* his citation counts."

Holywell was unsurprised. "Pretty shrewd, that's for sure. He knows the universities are using those numbers to measure impact."

"And he knows where *he* wants to go." Mary smiled slyly. "Perhaps we should have him give a seminar to our staff."

Holywell chuckled. "They *could* use better citation counts!" He rose, and Mary did as well. "You know, perhaps I should have confronted him about that newspaper article after all. If he thinks he can get away with doing stuff like that, he'll just keep doing it."

"That's the problem," Mary said, following him out of the office. "I don't believe Charles thinks he's getting away with anything. You have to realize what you're doing is wrong to think that. You're going to talk to him?"

"Right now," Holywell said grimly. "Wish me luck."

"Good luck."

Mary headed toward the stairs, while Holywell marched down the corridor. He entered room 405 without knocking and found Joanne behind a computer, Charles pacing behind her and speaking rapidly. He fell quiet when he saw Holywell.

"Hi, John," Joanne said, her fingers paused over the keyboard.

"Hello, Joanne," Holywell said, his voice maybe a touch louder than usual. "Charles, what have you been up to this week?"

Charles swallowed, his Adam's apple bobbing up and down. "Well, I've mailed out the Triggle 3.0 release."

Joanne's head jerked up. "Did you say you've—"

"Yeah, I knew you were nearly finished, so I thought I'd save you some work."

"You..." Joanne's mouth opened and closed. She turned back to Holywell. "John, I didn't know—"

"I know, Joanne," Holywell said, his gaze fixed on Charles. "Charles, you can't make a major decision like that. You're not responsible for communications. Anyway, it's not *your* project."

"I was just trying to help Joanne," Charles protested. "I know she's busy with the...with her..." He gestured vaguely at Joanne's now impossibly large belly, and Holywell fought back a groan.

"Baby?" Joanne said flatly.

Charles wrinkled his nose. "Look, a lot of people have been asking me about my new ideas for Triggle, and they want the most recent version."

"Is that right?" Joanne smiled at him, her eyes glinting. "Do tell us more about *your* ideas."

Holywell felt a savage surge of pleasure as he watched Charles squirm.

"Um, well," Charles stammered, "I've been thinking

about how to search for strings in the Triggle database."

"Yes?" Holywell said.

"Well, people want to find things..."

"Yes?" Joanne said. She met Holywell's gaze, and they shared a smile.

"And, well..." Charles chewed his lip. Then his face lit up. "How about I draft a paper for you to look at? I've been doing quite a lot of reading."

"Have you looked at the Cobra code in Triggle?" Joanne asked.

"Yeah, but I don't know Cobra."

Joanne rolled her eyes. "Sooner or later you'll have to learn it if you want to contribute to Triggle. Good thing you have that first class degree, right?"

"Listen, Charles," Holywell said, keeping his voice low and steady. "You're really getting on people's nerves. You had no right to take control of the project. I'm the chief investigator, and Joanne is the project lead."

Charles's eyes were wide. "I'm trying to help, Prof! I don't know why you're making such a big deal about this."

Holywell took a deep breath. "No more press releases," he said firmly. "And no more newspaper articles about how you run the whole university from a broom closet!"

And he strode out of the room before Charles could respond.

Joanne sighed and stretched, rubbing her lower back. For a moment, neither of them spoke.

"Look, Joanne, I'm really sorry about releasing Triggle," Charles said finally. "I didn't mean to stomp on your turf."

Joanne shrugged. "We all make mistakes."

"Right. But I really was just trying to help you."

"Mm-hmm."

"That's what we do, right? Help each other out. One favor for another."

Joanne swiveled around in her chair and eyed him. "What do you want, Charles?"

Charles's expression brightened. "Well, since you asked—you've probably heard Prof going on about simulating things? I don't think he's going to let me get away without building a simulation."

"He's right," Joanne said. "A simulation lets you control the experiments."

"Yeah, he seems to think it's like flying for some reason."

Joanne's brow furrowed. "It's just good science, Charles."

"Right. The thing is...I'm not sure how to write a simulator. I thought you might be able to give me a leg up."

"Really?" Joanne sounded surprised. "Didn't you study that in Tennessee?"

Charles shrugged. "I think it was an elective. I don't remember actually taking it."

"Strange." Now Joanne seemed as though she was

trying not to laugh. "You could write your own simulator, but it would be better to build on an existing one. Hasn't Amanda Rouge got a package that you could adapt?"

Charles pulled up a chair next to hers, sat down, and leaned forward with his elbows on his knees.

"I think it'd be better if we wrote our own," he said eagerly. "We want people to think of us, not Amanda, when they need a simulator. You're already known for your work, but me? I'm a nobody."

"Hmm." Joanne scooted her chair away an inch or so. "How about I loan you a book, and you can give it a go yourself?"

"I was hoping you might be able to help me with it," Charles said. "You're a really good programmer, Joanne."

Joanne studied him, her expression uncertain.

"And smart," he added for good measure.

After a moment, Joanne sighed. "I've written some code you could build on, I suppose."

Charles sprang up out of his chair. "Great!"

"It's in Basic, so you should be able to actually understand it," Joanne added under her breath.

"Do you have some time now?" Charles asked. "We could get a start on it."

"Oh, not really," Joanne said, glancing at the clock on the wall. "It's almost—"

"Please? Fifteen minutes?"

Joanne exhaled. "Fine." She scooted closer to her computer, and Charles hovered behind her.

"I think it's really important that we make it extensible," Charles said as she began to type. "That way others can build on our code."

"Amanda's tool is extensible," Joanne pointed out.

"Yeah, but hers is written in Cobra. This'll be in Basic. It'll probably be much more popular."

"That's really not a very good reason for writing your own code, Charles..."

Joanne's fingers flew over the keyboard as Charles watched.

"This is so cool," he said. "We'll be famous."

"Fame and glory," Joanne muttered. "That's why I got into this business, alright."

"I'll tell you what," Charles said, straightening up. "While you work on the coding, I'll start a paper."

Joanne's fingers fell still. "I'm not sure, Charles. John said—"

"I'll meet you in your office next Wednesday, say eleven? Great! See you!"

And Charles Mittleman was gone, leaving a perplexed Joanne alone at the computer.

Chapter 5

Deep breaths, John. Be patient.

Holywell stacked several pages on his desk as Charles entered his office. "You wanted to see me, Prof?"

"I did." Holywell attempted a smile and gestured at the chair opposite him. "I've just been reviewing your paper on the simulation. I'm pleased you decided to do one after all."

Charles nodded. "Did I tell you I've been working with Joanne?"

Holywell was startled. "Oh. You asked her for some guidance?"

"We make a great team," Charles said enthusiastically. "She's doing some of the coding, and I wrote the paper. It's due for the conference tomorrow."

"Joanne's pretty busy with Triggle, you know," Holywell said. "And she's due to drop a baby soon!"

"She wanted to help me," Charles replied with a shrug. "Anyway...is that my paper?"

He pointed to the stack of papers on Holywell's desk.

"Yes." Holywell straightened up. "I read it, and, well...it needs an awful lot of work, Charles. You've got a record number of split infinitives here. And to be honest, the expression is terrible."

Charles's shoulders slumped. "Oh."

"You're hyping things up way too much. You really need to be more objective. Just because the press is claiming the Internet will solve all of the world's problems doesn't mean we should."

"But we have to be thought leaders!" Charles leaned forward, that slightly manic gleam back in his eyes. "We need to be visionary."

"Being a visionary doesn't mean hyping things," Holywell said, tapping the pages. "Now, I've marked this up with my suggestions, and—"

"So you can rework the text a little?" Charles asked eagerly. "You write so well—you have some great expressions. I'd never come up with them on my own."

Holywell felt a flash of irritation. "Or we could spend more time on it, with you reworking the text, and just go for another conference with a later date."

"I can't!" Charles exclaimed. "If I miss this one, I won't have my ideas out there for another year. Amanda Rouge will beat me to it."

"Ah." Holywell sat back in his chair, studying Charles. Despite his earlier annoyance, he felt a little twinge of amusement. "So that's what this rush is all about, eh? Feeling competitive?"

Charles frowned slightly. "With Amanda? No. I mean, she's good, but my ideas are...I know we can overtake her if we promote our work more heavily."

"It's not about how much you promote it," Holywell said. "It's about the quality. But I understand, Charles. I had a...well, a rival of sorts, back in my PhD days."

"Really?" Charles looked surprised. "Who was it?"

"You probably don't know him," Holywell said with a shrug. "Professor Godson, at—"

"Middleton!" Charles interrupted, nodding. "Yes, yes, I know him."

"Of course you do," Holywell mumbled, then shook his head. "The point is, I know a little friendly competition can be a good thing, Charles. Martin and I certainly pushed each other to do better work. That said, I think you—"

Charles cut him off again. "How did it end?"

"End?"

"The rivalry," Charles said. "Who won?"

Holywell chuckled. "There's no winner or loser. I mean, yes, we did go for the same job and he got it over me, but I ended up accepting a much better position, and...look, that's not the point, Charles."

He paused for a moment, remembering the way Professor Wills had egged him and Godson on. Nothing extreme, of course, but well—the desire to be seen as number one in their mentor's eyes had certainly driven them both to do better work. Amanda Rouge was brilliant. She could probably take Charles down a few pegs; succeed where Holywell kept failing.

"I'll go over this again," he said, tapping the paper. "We'll get it in shape for this conference."

"Great!" Charles beamed. "You're the best, Prof."

Holywell smiled and dismissed him from the office. With a sigh, he took out a pen and began marking up the paper again. He would clean it up as best he could, but he didn't have time to give it the rewrite it needed for the conference.

Which was just fine with him. Let Charles find out firsthand that being pushy and self-promoting was useless when you didn't produce quality work.

* * *

The following Monday, Holywell was on his way into the lobby café when Charles came bounding down the stairs waving a letter.

"Prof! Good news?"

Stifling a sigh, Holywell pasted a smile on his face. "Oh?"

"My paper has been accepted. They loved it!"

Holywell blinked in surprise. "Did they? That was fast. Most unusual actually"

"We do have to make a couple changes," Charles said, tapping the letter.

"We?"

"Credit where credit's due!" Charles nudged Holywell with a grin, then consulted the letter. "We got three reviews - a reject, a weak accept, and a borderline."

"I can see they loved it," Holywell said wryly.

"Like I said, we've got a few changes to make." Charles folded up the letter. "I need to make some travel bookings. Can the office do that for me?"

"They can tell you what to do, but you'll need to make the booking yourself." Holywell glanced at his watch. "Now, if that's all, I've got an appointment..."

"I've already emailed Dr. Rouge," Charles went on. "She'll be at the conference, of course. I want to find out what she's working on next."

"Well done, now that's a great idea," Holywell said enthusiastically. "You could see if you could merge your work with hers."

"Uh, no." Charles shook his head. "I want to keep this separate. If I merge it, well, she's more senior than me, and I won't be visible."

Holywell fought back a smile. "Yes, that is a danger. On the other hand, the work might be better."

"What do you mean, better?"

"Never mind." Holywell gave his watch another pointed glance. "You can make a travel booking and charge it to my project fund."

"Thanks! I assume I can use first class?"

Holywell pushed the door open. "Yes...I mean, no! No, Charles, you'll fly cattle class like the rest of us."

But Charles was already rushing back up the stairs, and Holywell grumbled to himself as he entered the café.

Chapter 6

The Salad Experience was packed, mostly with a younger crowd clad in shorts and Birkenstocks, as if the place were a gym and not a restaurant. Holywell tugged at his tweed coat, which could no longer button around his belly. He scanned the tables until he spotted a familiar bearded face near the back.

"Martin Godson," Holywell said cheerfully when he reached the table. "It's been quite a while."

"Indeed." Godson grinned, half-standing as Holywell took a seat. His blue blazer and chino pants were perfectly pressed, and his penny loafers gleamed under the lights. "I was surprised to hear from you."

"Your name came up in a conversation I was having with a student a few weeks ago," Holywell said, nodding at the waitress as she set down a glass of water and a menu. "Thought we were overdue for a catch-up. How's Middleton treating you?"

"Very well, actually! Are you enjoying being Head?"

"Oh, you know," Holywell said, scanning the list of salads on the menu. "It's a mixed bag. You can't win, really—if you don't do it, someone else comes in and ruins your life, and if you do it, you ruin your own life."

Godson laughed. "Sometimes I wouldn't mind going back to being a PhD student. Life was pretty simple back then."

The waitress arrived to take their order—the Chef's Cobb Salad for Godson, and a Fiesta Taco Bowl for Holywell. When she left with their menus, Holywell turned back to Godson with a smile.

"I was thinking about old Professor Wills the other day."

Godson nodded as he took a sip of water. "Damn smart guy, but a bit scary."

"Remember the time we all messed up that assignment?"

"A tale retold a thousand times," Godson replied.

"He walked into the room and started writing on the board," Holywell went on eagerly. "He put the numbers one through ten on one side of a square, and the numbers from one to ten along the top..."

"And filled in the squares with other numbers," Godson added.

Holywell began to chuckle. "Then he says, 'this is a multiplication table. Clearly none of you can multiply, so please use this in the future!'"

He laughed, slapping his hand on the table. Godson shook his head and grinned.

"Now a tale told a thousand and one times."

"He was a terrific mentor," Holywell said with a sigh. "I doubt I'll ever live up to his standards."

"He was also totally naïve," Godson pointed out. "He played by the rules. Sometimes you have to break a few rules to get things done."

Holywell arched an eyebrow. "You mean like that time you improved my technique for compiling Basic programs and published it without including me?" He meant to say it teasingly, but even he could hear the slight edge in his voice. Apparently, the memory still stung.

Godson laughed. "As I recall, you were *trying* to write that compiler and ran into a problem. I came up with a much neater solution."

"We could have written it up together," Holywell pointed out, leaning back as the waitress set down their salads. "Good lord, these are enormous. I thought salads were supposed to be healthy."

He picked up a fork and stared at the heap of ground beef, guacamole, and cheese. Somewhere beneath there, he hoped, was some lettuce and maybe a tomato slice or two.

"So tell me," Godson said, stabbing a piece of hard-boiled egg. "This PhD student you have—what's his name, Charles, is it?"

Holywell rolled his eyes. "Charles Mittleman. He is probably the most difficult student I've ever had the misfortune to supervise. God knows what Professor Wills would have done with him!"

"Why, what does he do?" Godson asked. "I've seen his citation count, and he looks amazing."

Holywell swallowed a mouthful of spicy beef. "You've looked him up?"

Godson shrugged. "I saw he was attending the conference. I'll be there, too."

"Ah." Holywell sighed. "He looks good on paper, but that's about it. He couldn't have solved that Basic problem either, I bet."

"Is that right?"

"And he pushes the boundaries on everything," Holywell went on. "He only backs down when you yell at him—but it's only a matter of time before he finds another way to create havoc! The boy is a truck without breaks." Holywell spotted a slice of cucumber amid the beef and cheese and stabbed it viciously. "Oh, for god's sake, let's talk about something else before my blood pressure rises any higher. How's everything with Kate?"

"Oh, pretty much the usual," Godson replied, eyes on his salad. "She works, I work, it's all very civilized."

Holywell winced. Probing, he said, "Sorry to hear that. I, uh, I hear there was a bit of trouble with a student?"

Godson exhaled through his nose. "There were some accusations. Nothing held up." He met Holywell's eyes evenly. "She was just after a pass and decided to try something out on me."

"Oh, no," Holywell said, shaking his head. "No, no—was the door closed? I never close the door when I've got a student in the room."

"She claimed I offered a better grade in return for some..." Godson waved his fork and smiled. "*Favors.*"

Holywell tried to keep his tone light. "I heard you offered a good deal more than that."

"Did you?" Godson wasn't smiling anymore. "Nothing was proven. At the end of the day it's my word versus hers. It's up to everyone else to decide who they believe, isn't it?"

"Mmm," Holywell nodded, shoveling another forkful of beef in his mouth so he wouldn't have to answer.

Chapter 7

The next few weeks passed in the sort of blur typical of the fall semester, where the weather grew chillier and gloomier so gradually you almost forgot to miss the sunshine.

Holywell spent a relaxing weekend at home. He'd enjoyed a particularly excellent week at school, largely due to the absence of Charles Mittleman, who was attending the conference. Mary had even commented on Holywell's jovial mood.

"What's put the spring in your step this week, John?" she'd asked Friday afternoon as the rain pelted his office windows.

"Nothing per se," he'd replied. "It's just a glorious day!"

Thunder boomed outside as if to punctuate his point. Mary gave him an incredulous look. "I don't suppose your good mood has anything to do with the absence of your protégé?"

Holywell had shrugged. "It's been refreshing, I won't lie."

"Maybe for you." Mary had lowered her voice. "I have a friend attending the conference. She said Charles was extremely confrontational with Amanda Rouge during her presentation—loudly asking questions from the back of the room, talking over her, that sort of thing."

"Shocking," Holywell had said dryly.

"My friend also had the good fortune of being on the same flight as Charles," Mary added, shaking her head. "Apparently, he was seated near the toilets in the back."

Holywell let out a bark of laughter. "Bet he loved that."

"Complained at the top of his lungs about *travelling cattle class,*" Mary confirmed. "My friend said she'd prayed a baby would start screaming just to cover up his whining."

Now, Holywell stood at the kitchen sink of his two-bedroom apartment, scrubbing the pot he'd used to make spaghetti. His mind raced ahead through the week, creating a mental list of all the tasks he needed to attend to by Friday. He'd sent Joanne flowers and a note of congratulations on the arrival of her daughter a few days ago...but now that he thought about it, he hadn't received confirmation of delivery.

Drying his hands as best he could on a damp dish towel, Holywell made his way into the second bedroom, which served as his home office. The flower shop was closed on Sunday, but the guy at the register had taken his fax number as well as his phone number.

But there was no fax waiting. Sighing, Holywell logged into his work email. He sent himself a quick email as a reminder to call the florist first thing tomorrow when he arrived at work, then rested his hand on the mouse, intending to close the window—no reading work emails on the weekend, that was his personal rule. But then he saw the title of one of the unopened emails. *Re: Charles Mittleman.*

The email was from George Sunders at the University of Washington. Holywell clicked it open with no small amount of dread and began to read.

Dear Professor Holywell,

I hope this message finds you well. As you may know, I am the chair of the steering committee of the annual Internet computing workshop. I am extremely upset and angry to find that material from our call for papers has been copied in the call for papers for your workshop by Charles Mittleman, a PhD student in your program. This is totally inappropriate. To copy the description of our workshop to use to attract papers for another workshop is unethical. I am giving you the benefit of the doubt and assuming you knew nothing of your student's actions while he was at the conference last week. I suggest you have a talk with him, and I expect this won't happen in the future.

Best,

Professor Sunders

By the time Holywell finished reading, his face felt as though it was on fire. His fingers trembled with righteous indignation as he closed his account.

So much for his good mood.

* * *

The next morning, Holywell arrived at work half an hour early. His eyelids scratched like sandpaper, thanks to a nearly sleepless night. He'd tossed and turned for hours, mentally reading Charles the riot act.

When he spotted the gangly boy ducking into room 405 down the hall, he almost thought he'd imagined him.

"Charles!" Holywell barked, perhaps louder than was necessary.

A moment later, Charles poked his head out the door. "Yes? Oh, hey Prof!"

Holywell gritted his teeth. "A word in my office. Now."

He unlocked his office door and forced himself to breathe slowly as he shrugged off his coat and set down his briefcase. He settled into his chair as Charles walked in, looking uncharacteristically nervous.

"You wanted to see me?"

"Yes, come in." Holywell stretched his lips into what he knew must be a rather frightening smile. "How did the conference go?"

Charles lit up. "Really well! I spoke with a lot of people. They're going to use my simulator. I think I've overtaken Amanda Rouge! It was much easier than I thought it would be"

"Hmm. Did you get to speak with her?"

"Yes, we talked about her work," Charles replied

with an airy, dismissive tone. "I sent her some suggestions."

"That sounds rather aggressive."

"Nah. I just pointed out that our work was already available and much more powerful."

Holywell felt a fresh wave of humiliation. "Did you? And you didn't stop to think about how that might sound?"

Charles looked bewildered. "No. What's the problem?"

"Charles, you'll get known as someone who only pushes his own barrow. And we need to have a talk." Holywell continued speaking as he powered on his desktop. "I got an email from George Sunders over the weekend. He claims you copied material from their call for papers for our workshop. Is this true?"

Charles wrinkled his brow. "I wouldn't say copied. I saw their topic and it inspired me."

"But you..." Holywell trailed off, staring at his screen. A new email sat in his inbox, this one from Professor Jim Miller at Rhodes.

The title was *Re: Charles Mittleman.*

Holywell began to wonder if he was trapped in some nightmare. Maybe he was still in bed. Maybe there'd been something wrong with the spaghetti. Had he checked the expiration date on the jar of alfredo sauce? Charles continued rambling as Holywell clicked open the new email and skimmed the contents.

"Charles," he said when he finished. The word

came out strained and soft, but Charles fell silent. "Did you visit Jim Miller's lab after the conference?"

Charles swallowed. "Yes. I thought it'd be good to see what they're doing next."

Holywell kept his eyes on the email as he spoke, his words slow and measured. "He claims that you took it upon yourself to review a draft paper they had lying around the lab."

"Oh, I did look at some stuff they had, yeah."

Holywell faced him. "You mean, they *showed* you a paper?"

"There was a paper sitting on an unattended desk," Charles replied, wide-eyed. "I thought it'd be okay to look at it."

"Did it ever occur to you that they didn't want you to look at it?" Holywell said in disbelief. He jabbed a finger at his screen. "And is it true that you then wrote some comments on it? You *gave them your critique*?"

Charles laughed. "You wouldn't believe it, Prof! The paper was really undeveloped. And some of the expression was terrible. I thought they might appreciate some advice—just like you've helped me. They split their infinitives! Can you believe it? It was—"

"Charles, it's my *job* to help you, but I don't just take stuff off your desk uninvited."

"But my comments were correct."

Holywell squeezed his eyes closed briefly. "That's not for you to decide. You can't just invade their space and take charge. Professor Miller is furious. How do you think this reflects on me?"

"But—"

"You're my PhD student. They must think that's how we behave over here!"

"I really don't see what all the fuss is about."

"That's just not the way it's done!" Holywell cried. "You're a *junior* PhD student, and you can't just barge into someone's lab and take over. Honestly, it's bad enough that you do it here!"

Charles frowned. "What do you mean? I'm a team member—"

"Who is always telling everyone else what to do! And I've yet to see any evidence that you can do anything on your own. Now, I don't want to have any more complaints. You will write to Professor Miller and apologize. Professor Sunders as well."

"If you think it's that important," Charles said, in a tone that clearly implied he saw no significance whatsoever.

"I do think it's *that important.* How am I going to find examiners for your thesis? You're systematically going around pissing people off!"

"I don't think they're pissed off."

"Well, they are." Holywell stood up. "If you keep this up, I'll ask someone else to supervise you."

Charles opened his mouth, then appeared to think better of it. He shrugged and slipped out of the office, closing the door behind him.

Holywell slumped back down in his chair. He felt all the anger drain away, leaving him with a feeling of complete and total helplessness. Charles clearly didn't see his actions as problematic. He would apologize to the professors he offended—as least, as much as he was capable of apologizing—but then he would no doubt repeat the same behavior.

Or perhaps his behavior would get even worse.

What more could Holywell do? What more could he say? He had never been so forceful with a student before, but his words obviously hadn't gotten through to the boy. Holywell wasn't sure anyone *could* get through to him. Not even Professor Wills.

Or maybe Holywell was just a failure of a mentor.

He sighed, rubbing his gritty eyes. As Charles's supervisor, he had a moral obligation to get him through his degree. But he did *not* have an obligation to fix the boy's personality. All Holywell wanted was for Charles Mittleman to finish his PhD and get as far away from Northwest as possible.

His gaze shifted to his desktop screen, where he could practically feel the angry glares of Professors Sunders and Miller. Hanging his head in defeat, Holywell picked up the phone receiver and began to dial. He had a few extremely embarrassing phone calls to make.

Chapter 8

The Pacific Northwest suffered a particularly long winter that year, medicating their lack of vitamin D with extra shots of espresso. Summer caused a sort of delirium as scantily clad bodies crowded Alki Beach, basking in the sunshine. Another fall arrived, bringing chilly temperatures and constantly cloudy skies and the threat of another miserable winter.

Charles Mittleman sat hunched behind his computer in his apartment. Through the window, he saw the blond woman in the opposite building pop a tape into her VCR and begin stretching. With a sigh, he reached up and closed the blinds.

"I finished my thesis ages ago," he muttered to Sophie, who was curled up on the futon and grooming herself. "*Ages.* I could've written four more by now, while the examiners take their sweet time with that one. It's absurd. I mean, it's unprofessional, don't you think?"

Sophie finished with her hind leg and set to work on her paws.

Charles refreshed his inbox for the hundredth time. He'd sent his CV out to no less than thirty contacts in the last few weeks, and not a single bite. It didn't make sense. No way were these companies getting applications from PhDs who looked better on paper than he did. Maybe his email service had some sort of virus, he thought.

Or maybe Professor Holywell had been right. *You're systematically going around pissing people off!* At the time, Charles had thought his professor was overreacting. If his colleagues were so offended by Charles' suggestions, well, that just suggested a lack of humility on their part, didn't it? He'd only been trying to help.

Charles leaned back in his chair and grimaced. Perhaps he should have realized how sensitive people in this industry could be. Perhaps—

His phone rang, a shrill jangle that pierced through these dim thoughts. Charles nearly toppled over in his chair in his haste to answer. "Yes, hello? Charles Mittleman!"

"Charles! This is Martin Godson at Middleton. We met a few months back at the conference?"

"Yes, sir!" Charles sat up straight, his pulse racing. "I assume you're calling because you received my CV?"

Godson chuckled. "As a matter of fact, I am. Would you be available to meet with me Monday morning?"

A smile spread across Charles's face.

"Absolutely."

* * *

Holywell took a tentative sip of his steaming double shot and watched as Charles hurried across the lobby toward the café. Holywell smiled, and for once, it was genuine. After all, this would be his final meeting with Charles. The boy would be someone else's problem after this week.

"You've got my examiners' reports?" Charles said without preamble, sitting opposite Holywell and staring at the folder. "What did they say?"

Holywell cleared his throat. "Well, they've both said the work is a contribution."

"So they've passed it?"

"There were quite a few issues, and—"

"But they've passed it?"

"You'll need to work on—"

"Did they pass it or not?"

"Yes, they've passed it, but..." Holywell thumbed through the papers. "I told you it was over the line, Charles. You have to make some corrections, but nothing too serious."

"Ah, great." Charles beamed. "I'll edit it today and get it to the binder this afternoon."

"This afternoon?" Holywell almost laughed. "There are quite a lot of changes."

"I can do it."

"Of course you can." Holywell couldn't quite keep the sarcasm out of his voice. "But Professor Long still has to approve the changes."

"Sure, yeah."

Holywell closed the folder. "Professor Long must approve the changes," he repeated, holding Charles's gaze.

"Yeah, yeah!" Charles nodded, but his eyes were distant, his mind clearly elsewhere.

"So what now?" Holywell asked. "I hear you've been having discussions with Moonshine Systems?"

Charles's eyes came back into focus, and he beamed. "They're very keen to create a senior role for me. They even suggested I could supervise a team of twenty people."

"Is that all?" Holywell mumbled.

"But I think I have a better offer." Charles paused, and something about his expression caused a little shiver of dread to run up Holywell's spine. "Professor Godson's offered me a lectureship at Middleton."

He grinned at Holywell's look of disbelief.

"Martin Godson offered you a job?" Holywell sputtered.

"Yeah! I think a lectureship could be a great start. Professor Godson said with my metrics he could get me on a fast track promotion."

"Martin Godson offered you a job," Holywell repeated.

"So I'll be just down the road!"

"Oh, wonderful," Holywell said distantly. Middleton was indeed only a few miles from Northwest. Even closer than St. George College. "So close."

"We can collaborate. Just like old times, Prof."

Holywell drained his double shot and set the empty cup down with a thump.

"Can't think of anything I'd like more."

Chapter 9

Middleton University was a collection of historic Roman Pantheon buildings, stately red brick and white columns and gilded domes, all spread out over meticulously manicured green lawns and framed with oak trees and stately rows of white tulips.

And Charles Mittleman could see it all from the window of his office.

It was about time.

He closed his door and locked it, smiling at his nameplate before pocketing his keys. Whistling, he made his way down the corridor, nodding imperiously at a few PhD students as he passed. When he entered the meeting room, he found Daniel seated at the long table, fiddling with the phone that sat next to his computer. He waved Charles in and gestured for him to sit next to Anna, but Charles chose the chair next to Daniel instead.

Professor Daniel Williams was the chair for the Shaw Trust, a non-profit society that supported research projects with grants. Anna was an administrator, a rather mousy woman in Charles's opinion, but she was good at taking notes. She slid a folder across the table toward Charles, and he set his bag down before flipping it open. On the other side of the table sat a man with graying temples and steel-rimmed glasses and a red-haired woman drumming her fingers on the table with an air of impatience.

"Robin, Cheryle, this is Charles Mittleman," Max said cheerfully. "He's only joined us recently."

Charles sat up straighter. "Yes, I'm really enjoying the new environment. Chance to spread my wings and break free a little!"

"Welcome to the evaluation committee, and thanks for arranging the space for the meeting," Daniel said with a smile.."

"I'm looking forward to seeing which grants we fund," Charles replied. "There are some good proposals here."

"I've had Anna merge the reports already, and on the screen here is a sorted list," Daniel said, gesturing to his computer. "The top twenty grants seem pretty uncontentious—three good reviews for each—so let's agree on funding those and move on to the ones with an outlier. What do you say, Cheryle?"

"Sounds good to me," Cheryle replied.

"At the top of this list is the one by Godson," Daniel said. "Robin, you seem to be the odd one out on this proposal."

Robin nodded. "Yes, I didn't find it very convincing, that's all. But I can take another look at it if you want?"

"I thought it was okay," Cheryle chimed in. "But I'll admit, I'm no expert in that subject."

Charles cleared his throat. "I gave this one a high

score. These guys are doing some great things with Cobra. I know quite a lot about Cobra because we used it during my PhD. It's such a powerful and modern language. I say we should support it."

"Alright, I'll take a closer look at it during the break," Robin said.

"Thanks, Robin," said Daniel. "Anna, can you flag it so we come back to it later?"

Anna opened her mouth to respond, but Charles cut her off.

"I'm sorry, Robin, but I think we should just go with the majority. Cheryle and I both like it. Your review is clearly bullshit."

Daniel's head snapped up. "Charles!"

"Now hold on a minute—" Robin began, narrowing his eyes.

"Sorry about that, Robin," Daniel said, giving Charles an incredulous stare. "We'll come back to that one later. Let's move on."

Charles rolled his eyes and slumped back in his chair.

"The next one up is by Holywell," Anna said. "Another one with one very negative review." She looked at Charles, and he consulted his notes.

"Yes, I read that one a few times," he said, shaking his head sadly. "It's in the Internet search area. These guys have done some good work in the past, but to be honest, I think they're getting tired."

"I thought that one was pretty good," Cheryle said.

"It really doesn't have anything new to say,"

Charles said with an air of finality. "Anyway, I'd have thought they'd have more citations by now."

"I thought it was pretty innovative." Robin still sounded on edge, and Charles suppressed another eye roll.

"I know a lot about this," he said, looking at Daniel. "This idea was published five years ago. It doesn't have anything new to say."

"What?" Now Robin sounded incredulous. "Being able to compare whole documents for similarities isn't new?"

"Who cares if two documents on the Internet are the same?" Charles was getting impatient.

"I do," Cheryle said. "I can think of quite a few uses for that!"

Daniel leaned forward. "Well, we seem to have a genuine difference here."

"It's useless," Charles said loudly.

"It's not," said Robin.

"We really should be unanimous," Daniel said.

"I am." Charles said firmly.

Daniel and Anna stared as Charles got to his feet. "Excuse me, I need a quick break."

He grabbed his bag and the folder and left, the door swinging closed behind him. That Robin had absolutely no idea what he was talking about, Charles fumed as he headed to his office. He would have to have a word with Daniel about him.

"Charles!"

Charles glanced up as Professor Godson exited the room next to his office. "Hey, Prof!"

"I thought you were in the Shaw Trust meeting this morning?" Godson glanced down at the folder in Charles's hands. He quickly shoved it in his bag.

"Yes, that's right. Just popped out for a break."

"So how's it going? This is your first time on a ranking committee, isn't it?"

"It's pretty easy," Charles said. "Although that idiot Robin trashed your proposal. I tried to argue him around. We'll see whether I can change his mind."

Godson smirked. "He doesn't know much about the field."

"That's what I said!"

"Okay, but be a little careful," Godson told him. "It's good to get ahead, but people might think you're conflicted."

"Not at all! I think you're doing great work. Why shouldn't I say so?"

"Well—"

"The community's small," Charles went on. Anyone who knows enough about the work to understand it probably has a conflict of interest."

"Yes, yes, I agree," Godson said, clapping Charles on the shoulder. "I'm just saying, you're pretty young to be on a grants committee at all. I did you a favor, recommending you, and they know it. So tread carefully."

He squeezed Charles's shoulder, then headed toward the stairs. Charles unlocked his office and headed to his desk. He opened the folder and flipped through the grant requests until he found the one he was looking for. Quickly, he slipped the papers out and tucked them away in his top desk drawer. Then he closed the folder and hurried back to the meeting.

Daniel and the others glanced up as Charles returned, settling back down in his seat.

"I think we've got a reasonable ranking now," Daniel told him. "The only one not resolved is Godson's. Robin's still not sure, so I'll take a look tonight and make a decision."

Charles felt a fresh wave of irritation. "Don't you think Godson's proposal—"

"Charles, I said I would take a look at it tonight and make a final decision." Daniel stood up. "Robin, Cheryle, thanks again."

Both Robin and Cheryle nodded, avoiding Charles's gaze.

"Everyone, please remember that everything that has happened here is confidential," Anna added. "I'll need all copies of the grants to be shredded."

"No problem," Cheryle replied. "Thanks, all."

Daniel handed Anna his folder, then closed his laptop. Anna collected the folders from Robin and Cheryle, then held her hand out to Charles. He dutifully handed her his folder.

"Great meeting, guys," he said.

No one responded.

Chapter 10

"How is it March already?" Mary Long set a stack of mail on Holywell's desk. "It'll be midterms before we know it."

"Every semester seems to fly by faster than the last," Holywell agreed, flipping through the mail. At the bottom of the stack was an A4 envelope with no return address. Frowning slightly, he opened it and pulled out a document.

"Anything interesting?" Mary asked.

"It's a grant." Holywell blinked, staring at the front page. "Written by Charles Mittleman."

"Oh, joy," Mary said wryly. "Why would he send you that? Looking for a rewrite?"

"I'm not sure he sent it," Holywell murmured as he skimmed the pages. "There's no return address...hang on a minute." He frowned, holding the pages closer to his eyes. "Oh my god."

"What's wrong?"

"I've seen this text before. No, surely it isn't ...." Holywell swiveled around in his chair and pulled open the second drawer in his filing cabinet, rifling through until he found the copy of his proposal. Then Holywell slammed the papers down on his desk next to the grant, causing Mary to jump. "Yes, that little bastard has plagiarized bits from the proposal I sent to the Shaw Trust!"

Mary's mouth dropped open. "But...how would he even get a copy of your proposal!"

"He was on the committee!"

"John, that's..." Mary paused. "That's a serious accusation. The proposals are all destroyed. He wouldn't be able to keep a copy. In fact, my friend Anna is on that committee, I can ask her just to make sure—"

Holywell was too worked up to listen. "I'm telling you he's stolen great slabs of text!"

"He was your student," Mary pointed out. "Surely he picked up some of your expressions."

"I used phrases in my proposal that I've never used before," Holywell told her. His pulse was racing, and his face was hot with rage. "They're like a watermark. Anyway, why was he even able to access my proposal? He had a clear conflict of interest. He would have had to declare it up front."

"That *is* strange."

"You know, two of the referees reports were glowing, but one trashed it." Holywell let out a hollow laugh. "I read that bad report hundreds of times. I should've realized it was Charles who wrote it!"

"You can't know that."

"I read his thesis, Mary," Holywell said. "I just about rewrote it. His expression is terrible. That bad review had Charles Mittleman stamped all over it."

"John..." Mary shook her head in disbelief. "If you're right, this is a whole new ball game. He's not only trashed your proposal but kept a copy and taken key parts for his own use."

"He deserves to hang by the neck for that!" Holywell growled.

"But how are you going to prove it?" Mary asked.

"I'll start with a meeting." Holywell picked up the phone receiver. "Let's see if he can lie to my face!"

"Good idea." Mary stood to leave. "Keep me posted."

"I will." Holywell punched out the number with more force than was necessary. "This guy is just so damn keen to succeed that he doesn't care who he screws over. Even his own supervisor!"

* * *

By the following afternoon, Holywell had gotten his temper under control. Or at least, he thought he had. But when Charles Mittleman entered his office, Holywell had a sudden vision of himself vaulting over his desk and strangling the boy with his phone cord.

"Come in," he said instead, his tone flat.

Charles was hugging a book to his chest. "Good to see you, Prof! Sorry it took me a little while to get here. Traffic and all..."

"Sit." Holywell pointed to the chair, and Charles sat.

"I've brought you a present," he said, holding out the book. "I read it recently and loved it. It's all about karma. You might find it helpful."

Holywell did not accept the book. Charles swallowed hard.

"I've written an inscription in it for you," he went on, flipping the book open. "See? In gratitude for all you've taught—"

Holywell snatched the book away and tossed it on the floor. Charles leaned back, clearly startled.

"Charles, what the hell do you think you're doing?"

"What do you mean?" Charles glanced at the book. "I thought you'd like it!"

"Not that." Holywell exhaled sharply through his nose. "You reviewed the proposal I sent to the Shaw Trust."

Charles hesitated a beat too long. "I had nothing to do with it."

"Bullshit!"

"You don't believe me?"

"Damn right I don't believe you!" Holywell cried. "I got two great reviews and one terrible one. I wonder who could've written it?"

"I had nothing to do with—"

"Your hype is like a damn signature! I'd know it anywhere."

"You can't prove that."

"Yes, I know." Holywell fixed him with a stare. "Unless I lodged a formal complaint with the Shaw Trust."

Charles gaped at him. For a moment, and for perhaps the first time in his life, he was utterly speechless.

"If you do that, you'll drag us both through the mud!" he said at last.

Holywell grimaced. "I think the mud would stick to you, not me."

"I didn't do it!"

"You'd risk me complaining?"

Charles glared at him. "Okay, fine. It was me. Your proposal was a load of crap."

"Crap?" Holywell laughed. "The only good ideas in your thesis were the ones I gave you. You just played around and got others to do your work."

"You definitely don't want to go around saying that," Charles said. "It won't make either of us look good."

Holywell ignored him. "Recognize this?" He held up the proposal, watching with grim satisfaction as Charles's eyes widened.

"Where did you get that?"

"It seems not everyone at Middleton University is a fan of Charles Mittleman."

Charles scowled. "You've got no right to have that. I could accuse *you* of stealing."

"A bold accusation, given that there are sentences in here that have been directly lifted from *my* proposal!" Holywell yelled, waving the papers. "You plagiarized my text!"

Charles rolled his eyes. "You loaned me your proposals in the past. You said I was welcome to use them if I needed help."

"I didn't say you could use anything in this proposal," Holywell snapped. "And more importantly, I didn't give you a copy."

Charles stood up. "My metrics are already better than yours," he spat, abruptly changing the topic. "You're just a jealous supervisor."

Holywell couldn't believe his ears. "After all I've done for you—just get out of my sight!"

Charles ducked out of the office as Holywell flung the proposal at him. The pages hit the office door just as it slammed closed, then scattered all over the floor.

Chapter 11

By lunch, Holywell's blood pressure was nearly back to normal. He did his best to put Charles Mittleman out of his mind as he met with students and consulted with the Triggle team. At noon, he stood and stretched, intending to grab a sandwich from the café before his one o'clock meeting. When his phone rang, he wavered for a moment, tempted to ignore it. Then he sighed and picked up the receiver.

"Hello?"

"John? Martin here. Do you have a minute?"

At the sound of Martin Godson's voice, Holywell felt his face redden. So much for his appetite. There was only one thing Godson could be calling about.

Gritting his teeth, Holywell sank back down in his chair. "Yes, I'm glad you called," he lied.

"What the hell is going on?" Godson exclaimed. "I've just had Charles in my office practically in tears."

"I can't believe my own student would be so dishonest, Martin. You wouldn't—"

"Now hold on. What's he done?"

Holywell took a deep breath. "To start with, he reviewed the proposal I submitted to the Shaw Trust."

"How do you know that?"

"I got three reviews. Two were glowing and one was damning."

"So what? Happens all the time."

"The damning review was written by Charles," Holywell said firmly. "He must've known he needed to declare a conflict of interest."

"How do you know that?" Godson asked, and Holywell was pleased to hear a note of worry in his voice.

"I know his style...or lack of style. There's no doubt."

"John, John, John," Godson said in a patronizing tone. "You can't pin that on him. Lots of people have similar styles."

Holywell grimaced. "Martin, he *admitted it.*"

There was a pause, during which Holywell struggled not to add, *So there.*

"Okay, so he did the wrong thing," Godson said finally. "You can't ruin his career over a little thing like that!"

Holywell's mouth dropped. "*A little thing like that*? Are you serious? Academia depends on people being ethical!"

"Stop being such a purist."

"Did he tell you he plagiarized my work?" Holywell demanded.

Another pause. "What?"

"So he forgot to mention that," Holywell said. "Convenient."

"You can't be serious."

"He used great swathes of my text in his latest grant submission."

"How would he do that?"

"How should I know?"

"Calm down," Godson said in a low voice.

Holywell bristled. "I've seen a copy of his proposal, and it's full of my text."

"You taught him to write," Godson said patiently. "You should him your previous grants. Of course his proposal is going to look like yours. That's the point of being his mentor—he's cast in your own image!"

Holywell couldn't believe his ears. "You're *defending* him? Is that what you and I did, back in our day? Copy text straight from Professor Wills's stuff?"

"Look," Godson said. "At the end of the day, it's going to be your word against Charles's."

Holywell shook his head. "After all the years we've known each other..." When there was no response, he sighed. "I see. If you want to back him, then there isn't much more for us to talk about, Martin."

"Be careful, John," Godson said. "This may all come back to bite you."

"And you, my dear old friend," Holywell replied shortly. "And you."

He slammed down the phone.

* * *

"Mind if I join you?"

Holywell glanced up to see Mary Long holding a tuna wrap and an iced coffee. He forced a smile and gestured to the empty chair across the table. “Of course.”

“So how did it go with Charles?” Mary asked. “Judging by that uneaten sandwich, I’d guess not well.”

Holywell sighed. “He admitted to trashing my proposal. But he denies plagiarizing it.”

“That’s pretty serious, but it’s not enough to hang him,” Mary said before taking a sip of her coffee.

“That text is plagiarized.” Holywell slapped his hand on the table for emphasis. “I’ve got absolutely no doubt. Besides, it’s not like it’s the first time he’s plagiarized something.”

Mary began peeling the plastic off her tuna wrap. “But you’ll have to prove it, and you’ll just lose a year of your life. I just don’t know if it’s worth it.”

“I don’t either, especially after the call I just got from Godson.”

Mary blinked. “Martin Godson called you about Charles?”

“Mmm.” Holywell shook his head. “He argued that Charles was a promising academic and that I could ruin his career.” He dropped his voice into a lower octave. “*Of course, it isn’t right, but these things happen in academia all the time, John.*”

“I suppose I’m not surprised Godson would say that,” Mary murmured. “He’s not one to play by the rules, himself.”

“Do you think I’m way out of line here?” Holywell asked.

“Not at all. I’d feel the same way if I were in your

shoes." Mary paused. Leaning forward, she placed her hand on top of Holywell's, letting it linger a second longer than necessary. "But if you can't prove it beyond the shadow of a doubt, it'll all come back on you."

"So you think I should drop it?"

Mary leaned back in her chair, clasping her hands together. "You have better things to do."

Holywell rubbed his eyes. "I'm going to have to sleep on it. Or more to the point, not sleep on it."

"Distance yourself and move on," Mary said. "Look, John, what goes around, comes around. Don't forget that someone at Middleton sent you that proposal. You aren't the only one with an axe to grind. Charles Mittleman will get his comeuppance. And if we're lucky, Martin Godson will too."

"But when?"

Mary smiled. "Eventually."

Chapter 12

Charles tugged at his collar as he stalked down the corridor. Surely such a nice university could afford air conditioning? Seattle was under its first heat wave of the summer, and the temperature inside was unbearable. Yes, the thermostat in his office said 74 degrees, but it must have been broken. Why else was he covered in a thin sheen of sweat?

He knocked on Anna's door and entered without waiting for a response. "You wanted to see me?"

"Yes." Anna gestured for him to close the door behind him. "I've been doing the travel claim for the trip you and Professor Godson took to LA in May."

Charles tugged his collar again. "Yes?"

"I don't understand some of the transactions." Anna tucked a lock of blond hair behind her ear as she picked up one of the forms on her desk. "You rented a car in LA..."

"Yes?"

"For three hundred dollars a day."

"It was a nice car."

Anna gave him an odd smile. "The rental company told me it was a Mercedes sports!"

"Yeah." Charles shrugged. "So?"

"The university policy is that you choose the

cheapest car. I can't approve you driving around in a Mercedes when a Toyota would've done."

A bead of sweat slipped down Charles's cheek. "Why should anyone care?"

"Because it's public money, Charles." Anna spoke like a kindergarten teacher, which grated on Charles's nerves. "The community is pretty critical of the way we spend their money. Anyway, it's not for you and I to debate it—it's clearly in the rules that you signed when you got your corporate credit card."

"But it's paid now," Charles said, taking a step toward the door. "So..."

"You'll have to pay it back," Anna said. "And I'll have to tell Professor Godson."

"Oh, Martin won't have a problem," Charles told her.

"Yes he will, Charles. There are rules. And..." Anna shuffled the forms again, and her face turned slightly pink. "There's another item here. A meal at a restaurant called Passion Palace."

"We had dinner one night during the conference," Charles said impatiently. Anna's office was even warmer than his, and he could feel patches of armpit sweat soaking through his shirt. "Are you trying to tell me we aren't allowed to eat when we're traveling?"

Anna cleared her throat. "The bill was a thousand dollars."

"Yeah, we...we had a couple bottles of wine," Charles said. "You can ask Professor Godson about it."

"I will." Anna took a deep breath. "If it turns out Passion Palace isn't a restaurant, you're going to be—"

"Ask Professor Godson," Charles interrupted. "Anna, seems to me you're getting a little over your authority here."

Anna glared at him. "No, Charles. This *is* my authority."

Charles rolled his eyes and headed for the door. He needed some fresh air and a cold drink, and possibly a shower.

The moment he left, Anna stood and moved to the door, clutching the forms. She waited until Charles disappeared around the corner, then hurried to Professor Godson's office. The door was open, and she poked her head in.

"Do you have a few minutes?" she asked.

Godson glanced up from his desktop and smiled. "Yes, of course!"

Anna left the door open and took a seat. She set the forms on Godson's desk and took a deep breath. "I was, um, processing Doctor Mittleman's credit card statement the other day, and...well, there were some irregularities. Since you sign off on it, I thought I'd better raise them with you."

"What kind of irregularities?" Godson asked.

"Two things." Anna tapped the top form. "First, he rented a very expensive Mercedes sports car—red, apparently—when he was at that conference in LA last month."

"Shit." Godson looked more amused than angry.

"I told him he'll have to pay for it," Anna went on. "You can decide if you want to take it any further. Personally, I'd read him the riot act."

Godson nodded. "Alright. And the other thing?"

"The other thing..." Anna lowered her voice. "It's more serious, I'm afraid."

"Oh?"

"There's a receipt for what he says is an official meal at a Thai restaurant. It's way over the daily limit."

"How much?"

"About a grand."

Godson chuckled. "Must've been a great curry."

"Well, he says it was wine, but I actually suspect it was something a little...spicier." Anna's face warmed, but she met Godson's eyes. "It was at a place called Passion Palace."

Godson cleared his throat. "Sounds like a Thai place to me..."

"I'm not at all convinced it's a restaurant at all," Anna said.

"Hmm." Godson glanced back at his computer screen. "A thousand dollars, eh? Must've been fun."

"Corporate credit cards can't be used for...for this."

"No, no, of course not," Godson said hurriedly. "We'll have to call him in over that."

Anna swallowed. "He claims you were there with him."

Godson's head snapped up. His mouth opened and closed like a goldfish. "What?" he sputtered. "That...that bastard!"

"You should take this seriously," Anna said, lowering her voice even more. "That issue with the student hasn't settled down yet. You don't need more accusations. It'll all look pretty—"

"Shut up." Godson stood up, running his hand over his hair. "This is ridiculous."

Anna reeled back. "Hey, don't shoot the messenger!"

Godson deflated. "I'm sorry, Anna. Truly. It's just...it's all so preposterous! Who the hell does he think he is?"

"A guy who sees himself as pretty important," Anna replied. "That's who. If I were you I'd be careful about him."

"Right," Godson said grimly. "I'll deal with this. Thanks, Anna."

Anna hurried back to her office, relieved her part in this was over. Godson stepped out into the corridor.

"Charles!" he bellowed. "Get in here!"

He paced around his office, listening as the sound of footsteps drew nearer. Charles bounded into the room, and Godson faced him.

"Close the door."

Charles did so immediately. He was sweating profusely, and his face was tomato red. *Good,* Godson thought savagely. *You should be nervous.*

"Anna just came to see me about your credit card."

"I can explain—"

"Explain renting a Mercedes sports car?"

"I needed to get to a meeting across town!" Charles said. "Why does anyone care it's a sports car?"

"Oh, you're right, Charles," Godson said, his voice dripping with sarcasm. "I'm sure the newspapers wouldn't care that we were wasting taxpayer's money. I'm sure you could spin that into an article," he said, making it clear he knew about Charles's trips to the press. "Did it ever occur to you that maybe it wasn't such a smart move?"

"I don't think the newspapers would hear about it, would they?"

"Oh, so if we can keep it quiet, it's all okay?" Godson let out a humorless laugh. "Sure, let's keep this between us then. And Anna. And the finance branch. And HR. And who the fuck else do I need to keep it quiet from?"

Charles winced. "Anna said I could pay for it myself."

"Oh, you will." Godson crossed his arms. "Then there's the little matter of Passion Palace."

"You were there." Charles sounded like a petulant child. "I don't recall you complaining at the time."

"How was I supposed to know you'd put it on your corporate credit card, you idiot?"

"We were on business travel—"

"Yes, and all *legitimate* travel expenses can be covered!"

"Can't you cover it up?"

"No, I can't cover it up!" Godson roared. "You've dropped us both in the shit!"

Charles pulled hard at his collar. "What do we do?"

Godson resumed his pacing. After about half a minute, he nodded and faced Charles again. "What *we* have to do is .... You'll have to resign," he said briskly. "If you go quietly we might just manage to cover it up."

"Go quietly?" Charles looked stunned. "Are you mad? I'm the best thing that's happened to this department for years!"

Godson almost laughed. "I'm not saying you haven't improved our rankings. But this could explode. You have to resign."

"But—"

"And the bit about me being with you that night? You're going to have to drop that."

"Or what?" Charles took a step forward. "Martin, if I go down, you're coming with me."

Godson stared at him for a long moment. "That's very unlikely, Charles."

"I'm telling you," Charles said, his face growing even redder. "If I go down, so do you."

"Get out."

The two glared at each other for several seconds. Then Charles marched out of the office, slamming the door behind him. Godson stood there for nearly a minute, his fingers twitching at his sides. Then, making up his mind, he picked up his phone and punched in Holywell's number.

It rang twice, then Holywell picked up. "Hello?"

"John, it's Martin."

There was a heavy pause. "Yes?" Holywell said, his tone icy.

"I've, uh..." Godson exhaled sharply through his nose. "I've got a little admission to make."

"Really?" Holywell let out a mirthless laugh. "Let me guess. Our little friend is giving you grief?"

"Well, yes," Godson admitted.

"What's he done this time?"

"You know, I was always worried about the claims you made about Charles plagiarizing your grant."

"Like hell you were."

Godson grimaced. "If you want to make a formal complaint, I'll appear to investigate it. And..."

"And what?"

"And I'll come down on him like a ton of bricks," Godson said firmly. "He will never work in academia again."

Holywell was silent for a moment. "When do you want this complaint?"

"As soon as possible," Godson said. "If you can email it to me now, then follow up with a signed letter, that'd be fine."

"I'll think about it."

Godson fought to keep the impatience out of his voice. "John, please. We both need to get rid of this guy. He's the most ambitious asshole I've ever met!"

"Oh, really?" Holywell said sarcastically.

"I just worry about what he'll do next."

"I bet you do." Holywell paused again, then sighed. "Fine, yeah. I'll file the complaint right now."

Relief flooded Godson. "Thanks, John. Really."

Holywell hung up without another word, and Godson set the receiver down. He sat behind his desk and fiddled with his paperwork, glancing at the screen every few seconds. When Holywell's email appeared, Godson punched the air in triumph. He picked up the receiver again and punched in Charles's extension.

"Yes?" He sounded wary.

"Get in here."

Godson leaned back in his chair. He felt much calmer now. When Charles entered his office again, Godson offered him a smile that was almost genuine.

"Is the credit card business sorted?" Charles asked nervously, sinking into the chair.

"Pretty much," Godson replied. "I'd say we won't hear too much more about it."

Charles's shoulders slumped in relief. "Oh, good. So it's back to business as usual?"

"Not quite." Godson arranged his expression into one of grave concern. "I've just had a call with John Holywell. He says you plagiarized a grant of his."

Irritation flashed across Charles's face. "It's his word against mine. I think people need to trust their friends."

"Yes, they do," Godson agreed. "But I don't want to make an uneducated decision, so how about we go check your office right now? Looking for a copy of his proposal? I'm surprised you left it in your top drawer!"

Charles blanched, and Godson nearly laughed. *Gotcha.*

"As I said, you're going to resign," Godson said. "Quietly."

"And as *I* said, if I go down, you come with me."

"You haven't got too many cards left, Charles."

"Are you sure?" Charles leaned forward. "I bet the President would like to know what really happened with that student."

Godson felt a flash of anger. "What the fuck are you talking about?"

"In your words, *she got a pass and I got some—"*

"Shut up!"

Charles stood and glowered down at him. "I'm telling you, I will take you down with me."

Godson attempted to swallow down the rage welling up inside him. "Come on, Charles. I was just trying to make you realize how serious things are here."

"So you'll drop it."

Godson glanced at his computer screen. "I can't. Holywell's formally complained. It's in the system now."

"Well you'd better get it out of the system."

Charles sat down again, glaring at Godson. Closing his eyes, Godson tried to think. What now? What he wanted to do was reach across his desk and throttle the boy. But there had to be a way out of this, some way to keep this from turning into a wildfire.

"Tell you what," he said finally. "I've got a good friend at St. George's College. How about I give him a call and see if he's got a position for you?"

"You mean you'll quietly squirrel me away to some second rate college?" Charles snorted. "No way."

Godson forced a smile onto his face. "What if you got a promotion?"

Charles perked up. "What sort of promotion?"

"If you stay here, it'll be at least five years before I can get you promoted to full Professor, even with your metrics. How about they offer you a professorship now? I might even be able to get you an endowed chair ..."

He caught the glint of greed in Charles's eyes as he considered it.

"You think you can swing that? A full professorship at St. George?" Charles nodded slowly. "That might be worth it."

"Let me see what I can do." Godson gestured for Charles to leave, and he obeyed. On his way out the door, Godson saw him mouth the words *Professor Dr. Mittleman,* and he shook his head. The last thing he wanted to do was help the obnoxious prick. But what choice did he have?

Godson picked up the phone and dialed. Charles Mittleman was about to become someone else's problem.

Chapter 13

Holywell slept a full eight hours that night and woke the next morning with a smile on his face.

He had a quick breakfast of instant oatmeal and black coffee, and arrived at his office a full half hour earlier than usual. Whistling the jingle for a cat food commercial he'd heard on the radio on the way to work, he unlocked his office door and set his briefcase on his desk.

For nearly an hour, Holywell attempted to knock a few items off his to-do list. Then he gave into temptation and called Martin Godson.

"Martin? John here."

"Ah, John." Martin's voice sounded strained. "Glad you called."

"Did you get my formal complaint?" Holywell leaned back in his chair, putting his feet up on his desk.

"Yes. About that..." Martin paused. "I've decided not to follow through."

Holywell laughed. "What?"

"I'm not following through with it, John."

"*What*?" Holywell sat up straight and planted his feet on the floor. "You said you would. *You* convinced *me* to file that complaint!"

"I know, but in the end, it's your word against his."

"Did you check his office?" Holywell demanded. "He has my proposal, Martin, and he's not smart enough to hide it."

"I searched everywhere. He doesn't have it."

"Yeah, right." Holywell couldn't believe his ears. "So he gets away with it? I'm so glad we've been friends for so long, otherwise I might've misunderstood your motives!"

Godson sighed. "I've decided to let him go, alright? St. George College have offered him an endowed chair."

Holywell pulled the receiver away from his ear as if it were a snake. He must not have heard correctly.

"John? Did you hear me?"

"Yeah." Holywell put Godson on speakerphone. "I heard you, and you must be out of your mind. Is that what you call *never working in academia again*?"

"They liked his research profile," Godson said weakly. "What could I do?"

"Charles Mittleman never had an original idea in his life!"

"Well he's not my problem anymore. Or yours."

"Except for that complaint you had me file," Holywell spat. "I'm going to look like a complete idiot." He glared at the phone. "Perhaps it's time for you to move on, too? I wonder how much your Dean knows about all of this..."

"Are you threatening me? Because—"

Holywell hung up.

"Perish the thought, Martin. Perish the thought."

He picked up the phone again, fully intending to place a call to the Dean of Science at Middleton. But a knock at the door made him pause.

"Yes?"

The door opened, and Mary entered. Her smile fell when she saw the look on Holywell's face. "John? What's wrong?"

Holywell told her everything.

When he finished, he put his head in his hands. "I can't believe I let him convince me to file that complaint. I should have let it be, just like you said, but he promised..."

Mary was shaking her head. "I wish I could say I'm surprised."

"I'm going to call his dean," Holywell said. "It's the only thing I can think to do at this point.

"Don't."

Holywell glanced up in surprise as Mary placed her hand on his phone. "Why?"

Mary sat back in her chair. Her eyes flicked away from his for a moment. When she spoke, her tone was low and controlled.

"You remember a few years back, when I attended that conference in Boston?" When Holywell nodded, she continued. "Godson was there. We attended a few of the same seminars, had dinner with a few colleagues one night, and Martin had quite a bit to drink, and..."

She fell silent, and Holywell stared at her. His confusion lasted only a moment, then dread crept up his spine as he realized what Mary was getting at.

"Did he—"

"We had a personal conflict," Mary said flatly. "Let's leave it at that. And I called his dean afterwards. He didn't do a thing about it. He and Martin are pals, John. It's pointless."

Holywell let out a long, slow breath. "God, Mary. I had no idea."

Although the more he thought about it, the less surprised he felt. After all, it wasn't as if Holywell hadn't heard the rumors about Martin Godson. He remembered the annoyance in Martin's expression at The Salad Experience when he'd brought up the student who'd filed a complaint. *It's up to everyone else to decide who they believe, isn't it?*

"So that's it, then," Holywell said. He felt utterly defeated. "There's nothing we can do."

"Oh, I wouldn't say that," Mary replied. "I have contacts at St. George—Alison Simmons and I have lunch a few times a month. I'll give her a heads up about the bright young professor headed their way."

She stood, and Holywell attempted a smile.

"And what should I do?"

Mary returned the smile. "You should focus on Triggle. Especially that plagiarism detector. Clearly, it's something the world of academia desperately needs."

"Right. Thanks, Mary."

"Anytime." Mary paused in the doorway and turned

back to face him. "Be patience, John. Charles will get his comeuppance."

Then she was gone, and Holywell was alone. With a heavy sigh, he glanced at his phone before opening up his briefcase and getting to work.

Chapter 14

A brisk fall breeze whipped at the front door of Beantown, a popular café a block from the campus of St. George College. The door banged against the wall, causing a few patrons to jump in surprise. The barista, a lanky man with a silver hoop in his nose and several more in his ears, glanced up from where he stood pulling a shot of espresso.

"Would one of you ladies mind getting that?" he called to the two women seated closest to the door.

"No problem!"

Lindsay took a sip of her latte as Alison closed the door firmly. She glanced at her watch.

"Twenty minutes," she said when Alison rejoined her. "Then it's time to clock in."

"I suppose." Alison sighed, gripping her mug of chai tea to warm her hands, "I gotta say, this semester isn't quite what I thought it'd be."

Lindsay lifted an eyebrow. "I wonder why? Could it be that we've gone from having a head of department with perfect ethics and no ambition, to one who's all ambition and absolutely no ethics whatsoever?"

"I'll never get over it," Alison replied. "Mittleman's been here a year, and he's already been appointed Chair."

"The Dean wants to shake things up."

"I suppose he wanted to teach us a lesson," Alison said dourly.

Lindsay grinned. "You mean that fiddling your citation count is good academic practice?"

"The college is being reviewed," Alison said, putting on a fake, hoity-toity voice. "The Dean'll never become a President if staffers like us only publish one *quality* paper a year!" She lowered her voice. "You know, Mittleman told some young researchers that when they go to a conference, they should promote their own work during the question time."

"What?" Lindsay looked aghast.

"He said that academics were pretty easy to manipulate, and subliminal advertising was a great way to bump your citations."

Lindsay groaned. "So we'll have a whole generation of Mittle'men coming along."

"It works," Alison pointed out wryly. "He's got some of the greatest citation counts around!"

"Because he demands his students put his name on their papers," Lindsay said. "Even if he did literally nothing. That's against the Vancouver protocol."

"Doesn't seem to worry him."

"Remember Madam Ceausecu?" Lindsay asked. "The wife of the former dictator in Romania? She ran a research institute the same way. Insisted all of her chemists put her name on every paper."

"And look what happened to her!" Alison joked.

Lindsay laughed. "I doubt we can organize a revolution to get rid of Mittleman."

"I can't live under this for another three years," Alison said with a dramatic sigh. She drummed her fingers on the table, chewing her lip. Lindsay narrowed her eyes and studied her friend.

"What's going on?" she asked finally.

Alison glanced around the café, then scooted her chair closer to the table. "He's a serial plagiarist, right?"

"Seems so, but we aren't going to get far with things that can't be proven," Lindsay responded. "Once the evidence is gone, it's hard to prove anything."

"But if you plagiarize something, guess where the evidence is sitting?"

Lindsay frowned. "In a library somewhere..."

"Better yet, on the Internet." Alison raised her eyebrows. "Nicely archived and accessible and being looked after by people whose job it is to keep it safe."

"Okay..."

"I've got a little bit of a confession to make," Alison said.

Lindsay laughed. "I knew you were keeping something from me. Spill!"

"A friend at Northwest hooked me up with the beta version of the new Triggle plagiarism detector. I've already installed it on our server."

"The one from Holywell's group?"

Alison nodded. "It allows you to search for things that match in two articles."

"I wouldn't have thought simple text matching was very good for finding plagiarism these days," Lindsay said. "People have become much more devious. And by people, I mean Mittleman."

"But Triggle's able to work out if the ideas have been copied, even if much of the text is different."

Lindsay was impressed. "Pretty advanced stuff!"

"I tested it on some documents, and it's amazing," Alison said.

"Some documents?" Lindsay paused. "Are you saying...you scanned Mittleman's work?!"

Alison grinned. "It's off the scale, Lindsay. He's got stuff from all over the place. Holywell's a damn genius."

"Oof." Lindsay shook her head. "So what do we do about it?"

"Speak to the Dean, right?" Alison shrugged. "I mean, he'll have to act. This is hard proof."

"Absolutely!" Lindsay said. "Wow. Suddenly, I'm not dreading going back to work."

The two laughed and clinked their mugs together.

* * *

Later that afternoon, Alison returned to her office in a decidedly sour mood.

"Unbelievable," she muttered, picking up the phone and punching the numbers. "Un*freaking*believable."

The phone rang three times, and then a woman's voice answered.

"This is Professor Long."

"Mary! Alison here."

"Alison, I was hoping to hear from you!" Mary exclaimed. "How did it go?"

"Rotten." Alison took a deep breath. "I mean, the detector worked flawlessly, Mary. It's brilliant software, really. Mittleman's plagiarism is off the charts. I took it to the Dean this morning, and he said he'd talk to him."

"That's good..." Mary said slowly.

Alison twisted the phone cord around her finger. "I thought so too," she said bitterly. "But I ran into the Dean at lunch. He said Mittleman claims that Triggle is flagging things as plagiarism that are completely normal in academia."

"Seriously?"

"He says Triggle is being overzealous in claiming that things he's written were already published." Mary closed her eyes. "He actually implied Holywell was out to get him!"

Mary sighed. "Balls of steel, that one. So what else did the Dean say?"

"He said we'll just have to put up with it."

"Damn." Mary sounded tired. "You know, back when Anna sent John that proposal Charles plagiarized, I was naïve enough to think that was all the proof we'd need. I keep underestimating him. Or rather, I keep underestimating the powers that be and their willingness to ignore what he's doing."

"I guess that's it, then," Alison said, hating how defeated she sounded. "What else can we do?"

Mary was silent for a moment. "Well...we could take a page from the Mittleman playbook."

"What do you mean?"

"One of the first things Charles did when he arrived at Northwest was demand John give him an office with windows," Mary said.

Alison laughed. "As a first year PhD?"

"It gets better," Mary said. "When John refused, Charles went to the press. Had this reporter write up a piece about how he was this long-suffering genius running the Triggle team from his *windowless office.*"

"Good *god.*" Alison shook her head. "I suppose I shouldn't be surprised."

"It was pretty audacious," Mary agreed. "But maybe a little audacity is what we need to take him down."

Alison perked up. "You know what? I've got a good friend on staff at the Discoverer. The higher ed section."

"That could be useful." Mary hesitated. "Look, Alison, I fully support you doing this, but your Dean will probably know where the leak came from."

Alison waved a dismissive hand. She felt more energized than she had all semester.

"If it means taking Charles Mittleman down, I'm happy to take the flack."

Chapter 15

Lindsay glanced up as Alison burst into Beantown, her eyes shining with glee. Before Lindsay could say anything, Alison slapped that morning's edition of the Discoverer on the table.

Lindsay's mouth fell open. "He published it?"

"*All* of it." Alison waved at the barista. "Double cap, Steve! Thanks!"

As she sat down, Lindsay pulled the paper closer, her eyes skimming the article. "Oh, wow. Alison, this is...*wow*."

"Now we just sit and wait for the shit to hit the fan."

A high-pitched ringtone sounded, and Alison pulled her cell phone from her coat pocket.

"Something tells me it just did," Lindsay said.

Alison flipped the phone open. "Yes? Ah, hello, Dean..."

Lindsay winced, but Alison looked amused.

"Yeah, I saw...amazing, isn't it? Oh, I wouldn't have a clue." She held the phone away from her ear, and Lindsay stifled a laugh at the sound of the Dean's tinny wails. "It's a bit hard to sue an unidentified source, don't you think, sir? Mmm-hmm...yes...gotcha."

She flipped the phone closed and grinned at Lindsay.

"It's hit the fan alright."

* * *

John Holywell leaned back in his chair, an open book resting face down on his desk. The radio on his desk blared the morning news jingle, and then the newscaster's voice crackled from the little speaker.

"*St. George college academic, Professor Charles Mittleman, resigned today following a protracted enquiry into plagiarism allegations. Since the story appeared in last month's Discoverer, the college has claimed no wrongdoing, but did establish an independent enquiry. They released a statement tonight saying that Mittleman refuted the allegations, but decided to resign so he could spend more time with his family. Informed sources have highlighted the irony in the case. Mittleman is widely regarded as a thought leader in Internet search. He gained his PhD from Northwest University, where he was the project leader for the Triggle software that uncovered the plagiarism.*"

A knock came at the door, and Holywell turned down the volume on the radio. "Come in!"

Mary entered, an expectant smile on her face. "Just checking to see if you heard..."

"Oh, I've heard."

The two smiled at one another.

"Well, I'll leave you to your book," Mary said, glancing at it. "What are you reading, anyway?"

"Oh, just a book someone gave me." Holywell patted the cover fondly. "It's about karma."

Chapter 16

Charles Mittleman had been lying on his black leather sofa for nearly three hours without moving a muscle.

Sophie was curled up beneath the glass coffee table. She'd never quite gotten used to this newer, larger, fancier apartment. Although she'd left her mark on pretty much every expensive new piece of furniture Charles had bought.

"He always was jealous of me," Charles told her, for perhaps the hundredth time that morning. "Holywell. From the first day I met him, I knew he resented me. I should've listened to my instinct."

Sophie reached out and dug her claws into the hardwood floor, her expression serene.

"At least Godson took a hit," Charles went on, glancing at the copy of the Discoverer on the coffee table. "He got that complaint from Holywell and never filed it. Well, now everyone knows he was complicit in my so-called *plagiarism.* I always told him if I went down, he would too. Even though I didn't do anything wr—"

The shrill sound of his cell phone ring cut him off. Charles practically launched himself off the sofa and scrambled to answer it.

"Hello? Pro—erm, Charles Mittleman here." Charles listened, his face lighting up. "President Hastings! Yes, of course I know all about your college, it's highly acclaimed!"

Sophie examined the gouge she'd made in the wood, then dug her claws in again.

"Yes...yes...is that right?" Charles nodded, head nodding like a bobble-head doll. "As a matter of fact, I think I'd be the perfect fit...an interview, yes of course...tomorrow at nine? I'll be there. Thank you, sir."

Charles snapped his cell phone closed and beamed down at Sophie.

"Dean Mittleman. Now *that* has a nice ring to it..."

David Abramson is a professor of computer science at the University of Queensland, Australia, having also held senior roles at Monash University, Griffith University, RMIT and CSIRO. He lived through, and contributed to, computer science research and development that built the broader Internet as we know it (although he has no expertise in Internet search or plagiarism detection software). Purely Academic is a fictitious script informed by many years in academia, and doesn't so much set out to dictate what is right or wrong, but to engender a discussion about the type of sector that we want. His career as a playwright only began in 2013 when Purely Academic burst onto the stage at the University of Oxford, and while he has many years of experience in writing computer code and research papers, Purely Academic was very much out of left field.

Michelle Schusterman is the author of over a dozen novels, including SPELL & SPINDLE, OLIVE AND THE BACKSTAGE GHOST, THE PROS OF CONS, and the series I HEART BAND, THE KAT SINCLAIR FILES, and SECRETS OF TOPSEA. Her books have received starred reviews from Kirkus, Booklist, and Publisher's Weekly, as well as honors including multiple Junior Library Guild selections, the CBCC Best of 2019 List, and ALA's Rainbow List and Quick Picks for Reluctant Readers List.

PLAY PERFORMANCES

Purely Academic is a both a realistic and comedic dramatisation of the darker side of academia, including both personal and professional clashes in technical collaborations. It invites an honest discussion about professional ethics and practices today. What "persona" is cultivated by today's academic regime? With what impact? What does it mean to be an academic today? What does one need to learn to become one?

Performances

- University of Oxford Jan 2013
- University of Queensland Nov 2016
- Brisbane Conference and Exhibition Centre Oct 2017
- University of California, San Diego, April 2018
- University of Queensland, July 2019

Use in Research Integrity Training

Purely academic has been used as a resource in research integrity training. Using group walk throughs, the play promotes discussion on topics in both research, and more generally, academic integrity. Specifically, it has been used at:

- The University of Queensland
- The 2018 Australasian Computer Science Conference, Brisbane.
- The University of California, San Diego.
- Scripps Research, Florida.

Acknowledgments

I thank and acknowledge the following people

- Alix Phelan for her assistance in helping shape and finesse the play script.
- Andrew Watts from Conference Design for his assistance with the eResearch 2017 performance
- Cienda McNamara and Sarah Thomasson for directing
- Colleagues, friends and my family for encouragement on this project
- Dimitrina Spencer for her vision in staging an early version of this play in Oxford in 2013
- Jim Hogan for advising me not to give up my day job
- Jose Torero for supporting the first play reading at The University of Queensland
- Peter Arzberger, Joanne Wright and Earl Beutler for providing feedback on this text
- Reedsy for finding me an awesome ghostwriter
- Sarah Abramson for help with the cover artwork

- Sue O'Brien, Mike Kalichman and Emily Roxworthy for recognizing that the play could serve as a resource for integrity training.

CPSIA information can be obtained
at www.ICGtesting.com
Printed in the USA
BVHW041531301121
622873BV00011B/671

9 780645 321401